A GHOST AND A HARD PLACE

A REAPER WITCH MYSTERY

ELLE ADAMS

"Incoming!" yelled the girl I was supervising as she waved her wand with such enthusiasm that the tray of drinks spilled half its contents on its journey across the restaurant.

"Oops," she said. "Sorry."

Another wave of her wand cleared up the mess— which would have been fine if she hadn't forgotten the tray in the process. As the glasses toppled through the air, I whipped out my own wand and saved them before they hit the floor.

"Thanks!" she said, beaming at me.

I didn't return her smile. I'd been put in charge of watching the applicants to replace Hayley, the Riverside Inn's former bartender, who'd been sent for a long stretch in jail for murder. Unfortunately, there was a distinct lack of promising bar staff in town. We'd already dismissed one candidate for sneezing on the cutlery, and I was starting to worry this one would end up being worse than yesterday's, who'd given the wrong order to the notoriously picky Mrs Terrence and dropped a tray of appetisers on the floor.

"You don't have to levitate the glasses," I told her. "It's fine to carry them by hand."

"Oh, okay." She picked the tray out of the air and began to carry it to the nearest table. Halfway there, she tripped over her own feet. The tray fell from her hands, and I hastened to wave my wand again to rescue it before the glasses spilled their remaining contents onto the floor.

"Sorry," she said, catching her balance. Flustered, she plucked the tray out of the air again, leaving a trail of dripping water everywhere.

"Let me take that back," I said to her, shooting an apologetic look at the people sitting at the nearby table and waiting patiently for their order. "You remake the drinks, okay?"

As she ducked back behind the bar, I cleaned up the mess with another wave of my wand and levitated the tray back to the bar. As I did so, Allie Forbes, owner of the Riverside Inn, entered from the side door connecting the restaurant to the lobby of the inn. Her long, curly hair was tied back underneath her red-brimmed hat, while equally bright red socks poked out from underneath the hem of her cloak. "How's it going?"

"It's… going." That was the most positive thing I had to say about the current trial. Dropping my voice, I added, "She can't seem to go two minutes without dropping something."

"Ah," she said. "Yes… that's not what we want. Go on, send her home. The next one arrives in half an hour."

"Sure." I walked back behind the bar to join the girl, waiting for her to finish making the drinks before sending her home in case I startled her into spilling something else. "Hey. You can go home now. We'll let you know if you got the job within the week."

Or rather, as soon as we found someone capable of walking across the room without causing more havoc than a poltergeist in a museum.

"Okay, sure." She abandoned the tray, and I finished making the drinks and levitated them over to the right table—this time without spilling them on the floor. "Thanks for giving me a shot," she added.

"No worries. If you don't hear back, assume we hired someone else." I waved her off as she bounded away from the bar towards the door. She might not be good at the job, but that didn't mean I had to take out my frustration on her. I'd been on the wrong side of too many bosses who'd treated me like crap not to have an iota of compassion in these situations, and I'd also been shunted from one job to another throughout most of my adult life. Sometimes it took a while to figure out the right fit.

As she left the restaurant, I sighed and set about cleaning up the water she'd spilled all over the work surface. I wasn't the best at bar work, but I was even worse at dealing with people, living or otherwise. I'd hoped to find a contender with a more customer-friendly personality than mine who also happened to be suitable for the job, but that seemed too much to ask of the universe today.

Mart blew a raspberry after her as she left. "Well, that was a disaster. She's clumsier than a moon-drunk werewolf."

I ignored my brother until I was sure the girl was out of earshot. Not that she could actually hear him, since he was a ghost—a good thing, because he'd been flying around, singing at the top of his lungs and generally making a nuisance of himself in the background throughout her trial—but she could hear *me*, and I preferred she didn't know the dead were mocking her behind her back.

None of the other customers could see my brother, either, not even when he danced among the tables and made the glasses rattle. Seeing ghosts was rare for witches, but I was half Reaper, so I was more than used to the presence of the dead in my life. Especially Mart, who'd died an untimely death at the age of eighteen and had spent the years since then haunting me on a daily basis and generally making me look unhinged to anyone not in the know about my talents.

When the door closed behind the applicant, he added, "Maybe you should specify in the job ad that the bartender needs to be able to walk in a straight line without tripping over their own feet."

"We haven't had many applications," I told him. "We're giving everyone a fair shot."

"You must be desperate." He flew around my back and pirouetted behind the bar. "Can I work here instead?"

"Do you have a steady enough hand to pour drinks?"

Mart was stronger than the majority of his fellow ghosts, and his skills ranged from turning lights on and off to sending text messages to my ex-boyfriends without my permission. He also happened to be one of the reasons I'd had so much trouble hanging onto a job, which was one good reason I preferred not to have him as a coworker. Admittedly, my last job, at the morgue, had ended in disaster after the dead had decided they needed a say in their own funerals, and Mart himself hadn't even got involved. That kind of thing was hard enough to explain to my fellow paranormals, let alone to ordinary people who lived in the world outside of the magical community I'd grown up in. Honestly, compared to that fiasco, the trials had been a smooth ride.

"Sure." A glass floated across the bar, and the tap turned on, completely missing its target and spilling water all over the floor.

"Mart, turn it off." The flow of water intensified, so I walked over to turn off the tap and got sprayed with water all down my brand-new apron for my trouble.

Allie walked in behind me. "Everything okay?"

"My brother's trying to prove he's better than the people we've trialled." I turned the tap off with a firm twist. "He says he wants to work here, but I think you want a living staff member, right?"

"Hard to pay a ghost," she commented as Mart pulled faces in the background.

"I usually pay him in hot showers, but if you did that, your water bill would be through the roof." Yet another reason Mart was weirder than the average spirit. He liked to joke that it was because he'd only had me to talk to for most of the years since his death, to which I responded that it was no wonder I'd had so much trouble fitting into any community, magical or not. In fact, my stint in Hawk-wood Hollow was the longest I'd lasted in one place for a while, and I certainly hadn't expected to end up sticking around when I'd first arrived in town. The town of Hawk-wood Hollow was more haunted than anywhere else I'd ever been, and as a Reaper, I was a natural magnet for spirits. The whole reason I'd come here was to help Carey get rid of a troublesome ghost, and I'd fully intended to leave the instant we'd achieved that goal.

Instead, I'd ended up working full time at the inn while helping Carey with her ghost hunting on the weekends. I was also dating Detective Drew Gardener, who happened to be the chief of police in town. If anything, that part was more surprising than the rest of it put together.

Allie grinned. "You certainly keep things interesting, Maura. Tell your brother he can be on our reserve team if he likes."

"She doesn't have to tell me," Mart said. "I'm standing right here."

"Be nice." I used a towel to wipe the water droplets off my new laminated name badge, which said, *Maura Clarke, Staff.* I wore it with pride. "Like Allie said, you're on the reserve team, assuming you don't start pouring drinks on people's heads when you get bored."

If you asked me, it was harder to *fire* a ghost than to pay one, though I was one of few people with the ability to send ghosts into a permanent afterlife. Not that my brother had the slightest fear that I'd do that to him, because it was me who'd used my Reaper skills to enable him to stick around after death to begin with.

"I'll be on my best behaviour," he said. "Promise. Do I get a shiny name badge, too?"

I gave him an eye-roll. Ghosts usually appeared wearing the same clothes they'd died in for reasons that frankly even I didn't know, so he was still outfitted in the muddy jeans and scuffed shoes he'd worn as a teenager. "Sure, but only if you let me put your full name on it, *Mortimer* Clarke."

He shot a rude gesture in my direction, while I returned to watching the door. The next potential bartender would arrive around the time Carey got back from school, which would mean that I'd have company other than my brother to deal with whoever was next on the list. Or help me clean up spilled drinks, if necessary. At least I had a date with Drew to look forward to tonight.

After a few minutes, Carey entered the restaurant with her head bowed and her shoulders hunched. As usual, she wore her mustard-yellow school uniform, along with bright-red socks that matched her mother's. She walked over to the table nearest to the bar, where she usually sat to do her homework while I was working on my evening shift, and slumped into a seat. Her familiar, Casper, joined her, meowing a greeting to me.

"What's wrong?" I asked Carey.

She glanced up at me. "Someone else in my class has started a ghost-hunting blog."

"Seriously?" I said. "Who?"

"You won't know her," she said. "But Cris already has a bigger following than me, and she only started her blog a day ago."

My heart sank a little. Carey had been fascinated by ghosts and hauntings before she'd even met me, and her blog had been the reason we'd met in the first place. The knowledge that one of her fellow students—who, by all accounts, weren't particularly nice to her—had stolen her idea didn't sit right with me.

"Has she actually posted anything yet, though?" I asked. "Any real ghost footage, I mean?"

"Well… no," she said. "But she's popular at school, and everyone's waiting to see what she finds."

"Doesn't mean she'll do a good job at running a blog," I said. "Can she actually *see* ghosts?"

Carey shook her head. Most witches couldn't see ghosts, and fewer than average had that ability here in Hawkwood Hollow. Carey herself didn't have the gift, though her homemade ghost goggles helped her detect spirits, and I'd spent the last few weeks helping her find places where we could get good footage for her to post online. While there were ghosts in every corner of town, that didn't mean they were all inclined to cooperate with us. Most were barely strong enough to lift a feather, while others could levitate the furniture and rattle the windows. Carey was still perfecting her ghost-sensing cameras, so she could only pick up on the more extreme spirits, and I preferred to supervise where I could. I hadn't counted on someone else swiping her idea, though if this Cris person thought ghost hunting would be easy, she was in for a rude awakening.

"How were the new bartenders, anyway?" she asked. "Find anyone good?"

"Not great," I admitted. "The last two were duds. We have one more coming in any minute now, and if they don't turn out to be any good, we'll have to wait for another batch of applicants."

"Oh," she said. "I hoped we'd find someone by now."

"So did I, but I'd rather hire Mart than the last person we tried," I responded. "And that's saying a lot."

"Hey!" Mart said indignantly.

Carey's gaze followed mine when I glanced in his direction. She might not be able to see ghosts herself, but she knew *I* could, so she'd been learning to track their movements through my eyes. Casper was even more attuned to spirits, evidenced by the way his cat eyes followed my brother's movements.

"Anyway, forget this girl's blog," I said. "If it's just her friends who are reading it, then it's not the content they care about. Your subscribers are strangers from all over the country who genuinely want to read your posts. That's much more impressive, trust me."

A smile tugged at her mouth. "Thanks, Maura."

"It's true," I added. "Seriously, I bet this girl's just going through a phase. Once she realises ghosts won't show up and entertain her, she'll get bored and shut it down. You've been doing this stuff for years, and you have way more of a knowledge base. Also, you have me."

Her smile faded. "Sometimes I wish *I* could see ghosts. Cris… she said it didn't count if I couldn't. She called me a fake."

"Well, she's talking complete crap, especially if *she* can't see them," I said. "Pay no attention to her. If you like, I can send Mart to freak her out and make her regret asking ghosts to follow her around."

"I'd be more than happy to," added Mart, putting on a menacing grin. "Should I go and haunt her for a while?"

Carey's mouth turned down at the corners. "I don't think that's a good idea. What if she uses the footage on her blog?"

"Let's save it until later," I told Mart. "When Carey says so, you can go haunt her, but don't start causing trouble, okay?"

"It was your idea," Mart pointed out.

Allie returned to the restaurant and approached us. "Hey, Carey. How was school?"

Carey gave a noncommittal shrug. "Maura said the bartender trials haven't been great."

"And the next one's late," Allie remarked. "I think our third trial is a no-show."

"Should have figured." I wouldn't complain about not having to deal with another incompetent aspiring bartender, but I was already working fifty-odd hours a week thanks to the lack of other permanent staff, and it would have been nice to have someone else to take some of the pressure off so I had more time to myself. "I can wait for him."

"Doesn't bode well for his employability if he's already late." Allie shook her head. "I think people are avoiding applying, because… you know."

Because the last bartender turned out to be a murderer. Yeah. That.

"Not necessarily," I said. "I annoyed the entire coven when I drove Mina out of town, so pretty much all the local witches with a link to the coven are avoiding the place. I bet they've been telling tales about me to everyone else, too."

Not only had I exposed Hayley as a murderer, I'd also driven the leader of the local witch coven to leave town, therefore unintentionally making enemies of everyone in the coven who'd supported Mina Devlin. Regardless, I had zero regrets about solving the years-old murder case, which had seen Hayley lose her job and exposed Mina Devlin as complicit in multiple crimes herself. I wasn't shedding any tears over the departure of the controlling ex-coven leader, that was for sure. All the same, I did feel like I needed to step up and help Allie find a replacement bartender, and not just so I'd have more free time to see Drew. Not that I'd be complaining if I did.

"Maybe," Allie said. "Tell you what, you should go take a break. You've worked long hours every day for the last two weeks, and you deserve to have some extra time to get ready for your date."

"You sure?" There weren't many customers in the restaurant at the moment, but I felt bad leaving her alone, even if she did have Carey to help her out. We could count the number of guests currently staying at the inn on one hand, too, so it was fairly quiet at the moment.

"Of course I am," she said. "You've been working so hard lately. Take the rest of the afternoon off. You've earned it."

"Thanks," I said with a smile of gratitude. "I appreciate it."

I went to change out of my uniform, my heart lifting at the prospect of getting to go on a proper date with Drew for the first time since we'd decided to act on our growing feelings for one another. Once I found something to do for the next two hours, anyway. As I crossed the lobby, a teenage boy whose ghost liked to haunt the inn drifted over to me. "Maura?"

"Hey, Eric," I said. "Something wrong?"

"I need your help," he said. "My friend has gone missing."

"You mean that girl you hang out with?" I usually saw the two of them together around the restaurant, though they both insisted they'd never been a couple before *or* after death.

"Yeah," he said. "I haven't seen Lara in two days. I

know you don't like ghosts bothering you, but I don't know who else to ask to help me find her."

Frankly, it was kind of nice to hear that admission despite the bad news about his friend, because it meant the local ghosts weren't afraid that I'd unleash my Reaper skills and banish all of them if they got too close. I'd worked hard on making them see I was nonthreatening to ghosts while simultaneously making it clear that I had zero patience for being haunted either, so I was glad they'd been paying attention.

"Sure, I'll keep an eye out for her," I said.

As long as I made it back to the inn in time for my date with the detective, I might as well do something useful and try a little ghost hunting.

2

I followed the ghost out of the inn and towards the bridge arching over the river that cut through the middle of the town and had flooded twenty years ago, causing great devastation in the process. As a result, a large number of houses in the surrounding streets lay empty and abandoned, while the others had been rebuilt and renumbered in a manner that made them hard to navigate without a map.

"Where did you last see Lara?" I asked the ghost.

"Out here," he said, vaguely gesturing towards the brick building behind us. "She likes to wander around the inn a lot, but she isn't in any of the other rooms. I checked, and they're all empty."

I looked around the area. I could theoretically sense any nearby ghosts, but it'd take me a while to work through all of them to see if Lara's ghost was lurking among them. Asking the handful of guests at the hotel or the people in the restaurant wouldn't be much help either, because as far as I knew, none of them could actually see spirits themselves.

Outside the inn, a muddy trench filled the area between the riverbank and the side of the building, while the yard at the back of the inn ended against a brick wall that divided it from the neighbouring street. If the ghost had wandered in either direction, she might've ended up anywhere, and following on foot would be difficult. On the other hand, most spirits usually stuck to one particular area, like one building or even one room. Only the strongest had a tendency to roam. I'd have seen her if she'd been inside the restaurant, so that was off the list, but my best bet for finding her was to use my Reaper skills.

"Okay," I said. "I can run a general check of all the ghosts in the area, but even then, I might overlook her. If I wanted to track her directly, I'd need to get my hands on an object that was important to her when she was alive, if you have anything I can use."

"We both died in the floods," he said. "I don't know if there's anything left of hers… my mum moved away from town after we died. It was so long ago."

"Sorry." The town's history was brimming with similar tragic stories, as the floods were the main reason there were so many ghosts around. In the same floods, the town's Reaper had lost his apprentice and had consequently retired from Reaping altogether, leaving everyone who died in town from then on to linger after death. "I'll have to do a general check, then. One second."

Shadows swept out from underneath my feet, flooding the world. The inn disappeared under a blanket of darkness that obscured everything except for the glowing ghost of the teenage boy and several other spirits within range of us. While I could no longer see living people from this view, the ghosts' presences were like glowing lights in the gloom, while the outline of a door appeared etched against the darkness. Eric flinched when he spotted the door, which led to the afterlife—the permanent bit, from which there was no returning.

"What's that doing here?" he said. "I don't want to move on. I just want to find Lara."

"Ignore the door," I told him. "It shows up every time I come here, but it doesn't mean I'm going to force you to move on. I'll have a look for Lara."

I squinted into the darkness, focusing on the glowing lights indicating the spirits within a mile or so. My Reaper senses were rusty in almost all ways, but even if they hadn't been, trying to pinpoint one ghost among a thousand was like trying to identify someone through a blurred window. I focused on the nearest glowing light, which resolved into the shape of an elderly woman. Not the right ghost, then.

I moved on to the next—and out of nowhere, a blast of cold air slammed into me and jolted me right out of the afterlife. I staggered on the ground in front of the inn, reeling, a deep chill settling on my shoulders. I knew that feeling, though I hadn't felt it for a long, long time.

Another Reaper was nearby.

I stood completely still for an instant. With the exception of my brother, I hadn't set eyes on another Reaper in years, and the last place I expected to find one was here, in a town where the only Reaper had gladly stepped out of his role a long time ago. *Impossible.*

Shadows crept around my ankles again as I regained

my balance. I peered into the surrounding darkness, but the glowing spirits had dissipated. I saw no signs of the new Reaper either, so I let the shadows disperse again. The Reaper himself must be within close range for his presence to have affected me so strongly, certainly strong enough to be an active Reaper, though it was hard for me to know for sure when it'd been so long since I'd set eyes on a fellow ghost hunter. I'd left my own skills to lie dormant after my brother's death and my subsequent departure from the town where I'd grown up, when I'd left my scythe behind along with all my other tools for navigating the afterlife.

After so many years of putting as much distance between myself and my old Reaper apprenticeship as possible, the very last thing I'd wanted was to collide with another of my kind and drag everything in my past back out into the open again. Yet if I'd sensed the Reaper, they'd definitely sensed me, too. That meant I needed to find the newcomer before they found me first, and I'd much rather confront them here in the waking world than over in the afterworld.

I followed the direction the blast of cold air had come from and spotted a man standing on the bridge, half hidden from sight. He wore a long black cloak, standard Reaper gear, that covered his body from head to toe. His dark hair was shot through with grey, and I'd have estimated his age at between forty and fifty. The scythe strapped to his back banished any notion I might have had of him being here for anything other than Reaper business.

Yet if he was playing by the rules, he wasn't allowed to just wander into another Reaper's territory whenever he felt like it. Official Reapers had to get permission from their council before so much as breathing in the wrong direction, so if he'd been sent here by *them*, then he'd be displeased to see me to say the least. On the other hand, if he *was* a rogue, that might cause me even more trouble. If he'd banished the ghost, without permission from the local Reaper, he was breaking the law. No question.

Unfortunately, old Harold wasn't exactly known for taking the initiative. He might not even know another Reaper had wandered into his territory. Which meant I was the one who had to break the bad news to him, assuming he even cared. Tension gripped me, but I forced my breathing to calm and then strode over to the newcomer, waiting until I was directly behind him on the bridge to clear my throat.

The Reaper rotated on his heel, studying me with no surprise in his expression. "And you are?"

"Maura," I said. "I work at the inn. Are you new in town?"

"Obviously," he said. "My name is Shelton."

He didn't clarify whether he meant his first name, surname, or just a nickname, but it was a miracle he'd answered at all. Did I mention Reapers aren't known for their social skills? Years of dragging ghosts into the afterlife tends to erode one's patience for dealing with the living. Several good reasons aside from my brother's death had spurred me to give up on the idea of a career in Reaping and strike out on my own.

"What're you doing here in Hawkwood Hollow, then?" I asked. "Seeing the sights?"

The bridge was conspicuously free of the spirits I usually saw hanging around there. I hoped that was because they'd seen the Reaper coming and gone into hiding and not because he'd banished them with that scythe of his.

He grunted. "What's it to you?"

So much for pretending to be civil. I let my gaze drift to the curved weapon strapped to his back. He must have sensed my presence when I'd been in Death, so he knew perfectly well that I was a Reaper, but for whatever reason, he'd decided to wait for me to bring up the subject instead. Maybe he hoped I'd stumble and land myself in trouble with the council.

"We don't get many visitors of your particular profession," I said to him, refusing to rise to the bait.

"I can see that," he said. "I assume you aren't including yourself in that number."

I studied him. "Listen, mate, I don't know what you're doing here, but this is my home. I work at the inn. If you want to talk to the town's Reaper, he lives on the other side of the river, in a cottage in the graveyard. Number 42, if you're interested."

"Is that so?" He tilted his head. "Would he be able to offer me an explanation for the state of this town?"

Not before he starts throwing things at you. Then again, from what I'd seen of this guy so far, I'd be more than happy to offer him up for old Harold to use as target practise in order to avoid dealing with him myself. The grumpy retired Reaper would be even less thrilled to see the newcomer than I was—and that was saying a lot.

"Depends if you ask nicely," I said. "Whereabouts are you staying? Not at the inn?"

I'd know if he was a guest, and so would all the local

ghosts, for that matter. He must have picked another place to stay.

"You mean that hovel?" He eyed the building behind me. "No, I don't think so. I like to stay in an unoccupied room without any damp *or* the dead."

"There is no damp," I said, irked. "As for the dead, they'll leave you alone if you do the same. Works for me."

He had some nerve insulting my place of work and Carey's home, though it was probably for the best if he stayed as far as possible from the inn. I could just picture him striding from room to room with his scythe, banishing all the resident ghosts, and I hid a shudder at the mental image. The ghosts at the inn happened to include my brother. Strong as he was, he wasn't immune to a Reaper's scythe. It was bad enough that one of the ghosts in the area already seemed to have vanished, but I would never let this guy get anywhere near Mart if I could help it.

"That would involve neglecting my duties," he said. "It looks like you're already well practised at doing that yourself."

I folded my arms. "I told you, I work at the inn. You don't see a scythe, do you?"

"No, but I see an attitude I don't like," he said. "You're not a full Reaper. You're half what, witch? Did your coven kick you out?"

"No, I left of my own accord." I'd had enough of *his* attitude, considering he didn't even know me. "That is irrelevant, anyway. I'd like to know what *you're* doing in town so I can decide whether you're a threat to the residents or not."

Had he banished Lara's ghost? There seemed no

reason for him to get rid of one ghost and not all the others unless she'd done something to particularly annoy him. But I couldn't say for sure, not when I didn't know why he was here.

"I don't see why I have to explain myself to the likes of you," he said. "If you're not an active Reaper, then it's none of your business."

"Excuse me?" I said. "If you're here to make trouble for people in Hawkwood Hollow, living or dead, it certainly *is* my business. Are you threatening the ghosts?"

Instead of answering, he turned around and walked away across the bridge without another word. I watched him go, disbelief flooding me. Was he seriously brushing me off? It seemed my memory had not exaggerated Reapers' antisocial tendencies in the slightest. I debated running after him and demanding to know what in hell he was doing here, but I wouldn't have put it past him to take a swing at me with his scythe. Whereabouts was he even staying, if not the inn?

Reluctantly, I tugged my gaze away and walked back into the lobby, scanning the area for my brother. I was surprised he hadn't followed to eavesdrop out of curiosity.

"Mart," I said aloud. "Did you see that guy?"

He appeared in midair. "See who?"

"Weren't you paying any attention?" I said. "There's a Reaper out there. Look at the guy on the bridge."

He floated out the inn's doors, squinting at the retreating figure as he reached the other side of the bridge, then drifted back to me. "You're right. He has the scythe and everything."

"Yeah, he does," I said. "I don't know what his deal is,

but he's not friendly. He's also not staying at the inn, so he must have friends in the area."

He blanched. "Why didn't you kick him out of town?"

"I don't have the authority to do that," I said. "It's old Harold's job to deal with the other Reapers, whether they're Council members or not."

Though given his lack of attention to his other duties, I doubted he'd take it upon himself to do anything to the newcomer other than ignore him like he did the rest of us. While it might have been a laugh to see the two of them go head to head, I doubted Shelton was actually on his way to see the retired Reaper. Whatever he was up to, though, I didn't trust him in the slightest.

"Since when did old Harold give a crap?" said Mart. "He doesn't see himself as a Reaper at all."

"I know. He doesn't care." Not since his apprentice had perished in the floods, anyway. While that had worked in my favour when it came to him keeping my presence in town hidden from the Reaper's Council—not to mention the fact that I'd bound my brother's ghost to myself in defiance of half their guidelines—the stranger was within his rights to give him a tongue-lashing for neglecting his duties. If Shelton threw the rulebook at old Harold, it'd be entertaining, but if he returned with the Reaper Council at his back, I'd be their next target. And if he had them step in and take over the Reaper's duties, it would cause major upheavals for the entire town. Especially the dead.

"Want me to haunt him?" said Mart. "I can drive him off, no problem."

"Definitely not," I said. "I won't risk him using that scythe on you."

"I'll follow him, then," said Mart. "See if I can find out what he's doing here. Or where he's staying."

"Are you sure?" I asked. "If he catches you, you know what he'll do."

"He won't catch me," he said. "I can hide among the other ghosts, no problem. He can't banish all of us at once."

"He might try." Mart was stealthier than I was, though, for obvious reasons. Reapers could sense the dead, but if my attempts to find Lara's ghost had proven anything, it was that a high number of ghosts made it hard to pinpoint a specific one. That would be advantageous when it came to tailing our Reaper friend.

"I don't want another Reaper hanging around being annoying," he said. "That honour goes to you."

"You say the sweetest things." I rolled my eyes at him. "Just be careful not to get caught."

If Mart ended up being banished, even my Reaper skills wouldn't be able to get him back. Following Shelton was risky, no mistake. Lara's ghost had already vanished. Might her disappearance be connected to the new Reaper's mysterious visit to town? I doubted old Harold cared about one ghost's absence either way, and I had an inkling even this wouldn't be enough to stir him into action, but I still wondered.

Whatever Shelton the Reaper was doing in town, I was willing to bet he hadn't come for a simple holiday. He was up to something, and I intended to find out what.

3

While Mart followed the Reaper's retreating back, I spotted Eric's ghost hiding in the corner of the inn's lobby. I approached him, and he lifted his head, watching me with fearful eyes. "Is the Reaper gone?"

"That new Reaper," I said to him. "Have you seen him before?"

"No," he said. "No, but I sensed him. At first, I thought it was you, but he—he has that… that weapon."

"Do you think his appearance might be linked to Lara going missing?" I asked.

"I hope not." His voice quietened. "I really hope not. What if he's here to banish us one at a time?"

"Didn't look that way to me. Besides, that's not how it usually works." I tried for a reassuring tone, but my own mistrust of the newcomer seeped through. "My brother is tailing him to see what he's doing here. I can have a word with old Harold, too, and make sure he knows there's a new Reaper in town. But if you think he might be linked to Lara's disappearance… I need to know so I can confront him about it before he has the chance to strike again."

"I don't know," he said. "I didn't even know he was a Reaper before I saw the scythe. Is he staying here in town?"

"My brother's going to find out where he's staying so we can make sure he won't take us unawares." I couldn't do any more than that. The guy hadn't told me his reasons for being here, and if we came to blows, I preferred it not be a public event. I also didn't want the local ghosts to get caught up in the backlash. "I'll keep an eye out for Lara, too, but she might've hidden somewhere when the Reaper showed up."

"Yeah." He gave a nod, his expression brightening. "That makes sense. I hope he came alone."

Me too. I bloody well hoped Shelton was the only new Reaper in town, that was for sure.

Shadows crept from underneath my feet, and I resumed my search of the afterlife for any signs of Lara's ghost. The Reaper's presence seemed to have scared most of the local spirits into backing off, though, and no matter how hard I looked, her ghost didn't show up in or around the building. I dropped the shadows and walked back into the restaurant, figuring that bringing the afterlife in with me would dampen the inn's reputation as family friendly, to say the least.

Allie beckoned me over. "There you are, Maura. Are you going to get ready for your date with the detective?"

"Sure," I said. "Just got distracted."

"Nervous?" she asked in sympathetic tones. "Where are you going again?"

"A restaurant called the Hair of the Wolf." I'd never been there before, since I usually ate at the restaurant at the inn even when I wasn't working. Drew had picked out the shifter-owned establishment for our date, probably because it'd feel less like we were being watched all the time. Not that I minded spending time around Allie and Carey, but tonight was just for the detective and me. I'd made Mart promise to stay away as well, though he now had the new Reaper to occupy his attention.

"Ah, that's over in the werewolves' area of town," she said. "Makes sense. Maybe he wants to introduce you to his favourite haunts."

"Yeah." I walked towards the glass doors to the lobby, fervently hoping that *haunts* would apply only to Drew and not to the town's resident spirits. "I'll go and get ready."

I didn't normally put much thought into how I dressed —black jeans and plain T-shirts were my usual style, since Reapers tried to avoid drawing attention, and most of us didn't care much for fashion—but I made a special effort tonight. I even wore a skirt for once, which showed off more of my legs than I usually put on display, along with a jacket and heeled shoes I hadn't worn in years.

Allie beamed at me when I walked past her in the lobby. "New look? I like it."

"Thanks." I tugged self-consciously on the collar of my jacket. "Better hope I don't run into any troublemaking ghosts. I can't run in these heels."

I looked outside and saw Detective Drew himself approaching the inn. Like most shifters, he was tall and broad, though his longish dark hair was a contrast to the typical blond of the majority of his fellow werewolves. He was also out of uniform and dressed casually in jeans and a shirt that gave him a more rugged look than usual, accentuated by the faint traces of stubble on his face. My stomach fluttered when he gave me a smile as I walked out to meet him. "Hey, Maura."

"Hey," I said.

My heart swooped as his gaze dipped to my exposed legs. "You look great."

"You're not so bad yourself." I walked in step with him towards the bridge over the river. Night had fallen over the rooftops, and the dark streets would have looked eerie if I hadn't been used to trekking around creepy places at night. A few ghosts drifted past, which was at least a promising sign that a certain Reaper had left the area.

Hopefully he left the town too. I scanned the nearest ghosts in case one of them turned out to be Mart, but there was no sign of him among the spirits crossing the bridge. Nor Lara, either. Usually when I dated, I kept my expectations below ground level. This time, I really wanted it to work, and not just because my recent romantic history was downright tragic. That meant keeping away from any ghosts, including Mart, though I hoped to be able to snag an update on our Reaper friend from him later tonight.

Detective Drew followed my gaze back to the inn. "Your brother isn't going to follow us, is he?"

"Nah, I told him to leave us alone," I reassured him. "I made it quite clear."

"Really?" he said. "He's not going to barge in on us if he gets bored, is he?"

"No… well, he's kind of spying on someone else at the moment," I admitted. "But he won't show up in the middle of our date. I told him not to. He might like pranking people, but he'll be on his best behaviour."

"Good," he said. "Don't get me wrong, I know he's your family, but it's hard to tell someone to go away that you can't see or hear."

"It's better if you can't hear him, trust me." The comments Mart made about the detective were annoying enough for me to listen to, let alone everyone else.

Luckily, my brother seemed to have taken his quest to spy on the new Reaper seriously, because he didn't show up as we walked across town towards the restaurant. The cheerful redbrick building in the werewolves' area of town was bustling with shifters of all types. I peered inside first to check for any ghosts, but the handful of spirits hovering around didn't pay me any attention. So far, so good.

We picked a table near the window and ordered our meals in the usual magical method: by picking up the menus and tapping on our selections with our fingertips. It was a perk I'd missed when I'd lived in the normal world, I wouldn't lie. At least we were far enough from the witches' area of town that I had little chance of running into any ex-coven members, too.

"No ghosts in here?" Drew asked.

"None that are likely to bother me."

"Thought not," he said. "That's partly why I picked this place. Witches and wizards are more likely to become ghosts than other types of paranormals, aren't they?"

I raised a brow. "Have you been researching?"

"Purely out of personal interest," he said. "It seemed to me that I ought to get an idea of how Reapers operate if I'm going to be spending a lot of time with one of them."

"The Reapers don't typically let information about how they operate go public," I warned him. "You might find it hard to access anything substantial."

"You forget the police department has access to a lot of sources nobody else does," he said. "Also, we might not have an active Reaper in town at the moment, but we used to, and the police did consult with him on occasion."

I pulled a face. "Please tell me you haven't been asking old Harold about me."

"I haven't," he said. "Does it bother you? I can stop researching if you like, but I thought it would help me to understand how it all works."

My mouth parted. "It doesn't bother me, but I'm not a typical Reaper. I'm not even supposed to exist. There are strict rules against Reapers procreating with non-Reapers, and it goes without saying that my dad kinda blew that rule to pieces when he married my mum and had two kids."

Both of his brows shot into the air. "Does that rule apply to you as well?"

Heat rushed to my cheeks when it belatedly hit me what he was implying. Why had I decided to bring that up on our first date? Why?

"No, because I'm not an active Reaper." I looked down at the menu to avoid meeting his eyes. "I threw away my apprenticeship when I left home, so none of the rules apply to me aside from the secrecy rules telling us not to share our secrets with outsiders."

Drew wore a contemplative expression, as though he was considering a response, but to my relief, our orders appeared on the table at that moment. I dug into my pasta for a few bites before sidestepping into a different subject.

"Have you always worked for the paranormal police force?" I asked.

"Sure," Drew said. "I always knew I wanted to help people. Werewolves are generally raised in a pack, so we see ourselves as part of a group. That makes us a good fit for keeping order among other paranormals."

That fit with what I already knew. Shifters were pretty much the opposite of the Reapers, who viewed themselves as separate from humanity as a whole, paranormal and otherwise. We kept our distance, and it was a habit I'd found hard to break. Luckily, the detective was well aware of that fact.

"That's cool." I took another bite of my food. "I've never spent a lot of time around werewolves. Not sure why, because like you said, they're less likely to stick around after death and haunt people."

He seemed to consider this. "I guess we're pretty laid back about that sort of thing. Comes from being connected to the animal half of ourselves. We see death as inevitable. Not worth kicking up a fuss."

"Yeah, witches and wizards don't see it that way," I said. "They're usually the ones who raise hell and fight back when you try to shove them into the afterlife."

"Does that happen often?" he said. "I thought you'd never been an active Reaper."

"I'm not," I said. "Doesn't mean I don't occasionally run into a troublesome ghost who needs dealing with. Ghost hunting doesn't count as Reaping. Technically."

His eyes twinkled. "Don't worry. I'm off duty. I won't tell a soul."

"I should hope not." I took a few more bites, more to stop myself from running my mouth off than anything else. Maybe I should have compiled a list of suitable questions for a first date. So far, I'd covered Reaper procreation, paranormal attitudes towards death, and breaking the law. *Think of something less... provocative, Maura.*

"So, what else do you like to do when you're off duty?" I asked. "Aside from howling at the moon?"

He shrugged. "Running, working out, watching movies. I don't get a ton of downtime."

"Same here," I said. "I mean, my hobbies mostly consist of debating the finer points of Sky Hopper with my brother or watching old *Doctor Who* episodes."

"Is this a good time to admit I've never seen it?"

I feigned a shocked gasp. "Do you not get much nonparanormal entertainment in the pack?"

"We get some," he said. "You might've noticed we don't have much else going on here in Hawkwood Hollow. Including access to popular TV shows."

"That might change if we can get tourism levels up when Allie and I turn the inn into a haunted hotel," I said. "That's no excuse, though. You have the internet."

He grinned. "Then you'll have to show me someday."

"Please don't tell me you haven't seen *Star Wars* either."

"Okay, I won't tell you."

"*Drew.*"

"You sound so scandalised." He jabbed a fork in my direction. "You don't even get this worked up about ghosts."

"Ghosts are a hobby. *Star Wars* is a lifestyle." I gave him an eye-roll. "I *will* show you. Consider yourself warned."

"I will," he said. "How's the plan to turn the inn into a ghost hotel going, anyway?"

"Allie and Carey are talking strategies," I said. "We've

been focused on finding replacement bar staff before we make any other major changes."

"You still haven't found anyone yet?"

"Nobody with an ounce of potential," I said. "The third guy today didn't even show up, and the other two left much to be desired. And yesterday, our trial ran out hysterically screaming after one of our regular customers yelled at her. Admittedly, old Mrs Terrence screams bloody murder if her plate is the wrong way around or her tea is slightly too cold, but honestly."

"Sounds like a challenge," he said. "I'll put out word among the pack. I can think of a few of our younger members who might want the work."

"You sure?" I said, surprised.

"Of course."

Gratitude flooded me. "Thanks. I think the main issue is that the local witches and wizards have a grudge against me for driving their coven leader out of town. Even the wizards have stopped coming to the inn as often. We think they've started venturing into the Crooked Broomstick again, which used to be the coven's favourite hangout."

"Oh, the pack doesn't care about coven drama," he said. "We have enough of our own. I'll ask around and see if I can get any interest."

"Werewolves won't be able to see ghosts, which should help," I acknowledged.

Luckily, the ghosts in here seemed inclined to leave the living alone for the most part, and we moved on to more upbeat topics for the remainder of our date.

As I'd finished my food and was considering ordering dessert, the door opened, and Shelton the Reaper, of all people, walked in, scythe and all. Judging by the way people stared at him, he hadn't bothered using his Reaper abilities to hide himself, which he certainly could have done if he'd wanted to.

What the hell is he playing at?

Drew noticed my mouth had fallen open and followed my gaze to the Reaper. "Someone you know?"

"You know the person I sent my brother to spy on?" I muttered. "That's him."

To my utter horror, Shelton walked over to our table and stopped right next to the pair of us, making it quite clear to everyone in the vicinity that we were his targets.

I looked up at him. "Can I help you?"

He glared at me. "Don't think I didn't notice."

"I'm sorry, what?" I said. "Look, it might have escaped your attention, but I'm busy. If you want to talk, can you wait until after we're done here?"

Drew cleared his throat. "If you have a problem with Maura, then you'll have to take it up with me."

"And who might you be?" said the Reaper.

"I'm Detective Drew Gardener," said Drew. "Chief of police in Hawkwood Hollow."

Even *that* didn't seem to bother the Reaper. He barely blinked. "Charmed, I'm sure. This young woman is a troublemaker."

"Thanks," I said. "Why did you come here and interrupt my date? If you wanted to talk to me, then you might've stuck around earlier rather than marching off when I was in the middle of asking you a question."

"I had no obligation to carry on a conversation with you," he said, "but if you send your brother after me again, I'll have to take action."

My blood chilled despite my lingering anger as he angled himself so the scythe on his back caught the light. "If you lay a finger on him, then you'll get to meet my less diplomatic side, and it won't be pretty. Now kindly leave us alone."

He narrowed his eyes. "If either of you crosses me again, I'll ensure you regret it."

And, oblivious to the other patrons' stares, he turned around and left the restaurant.

Drew's gaze followed him. "Interesting. Is he new in town?"

"Unfortunately." I turned back to the detective as the door closed on the Reaper. "I can't tell if he's with the Reaper Council or not, but he stormed off when I tried to find out what he was doing here."

"Did he, now?" he said. "You didn't mention him before."

"I wanted to keep that topic to a minimum." I lowered my head, wishing the other patrons would stop glancing towards us and muttering among themselves. I would have bet most of them had never set eyes on a Reaper aside from old Harold. "You might've noticed he's not exactly personable. I only wanted to know what he's doing here. Maybe he'll turn out to be a friend of old Harold's who's come here for a visit, but I somehow doubt it."

His words about my brother had rubbed me up the wrong way too. At least he hadn't banished him outright, but Mart was good enough at being stealthy that Shelton must have been watching for anyone following him, living or dead. It was lucky for both of us he hadn't turned his scythe on Mart.

Drew's frown remained in place. "He isn't staying at the inn?"

"Of course not," I said. "He refused to answer me when I asked, but I hoped my brother might be able to find out by following him."

"Whatever he's here for, you'd be better off staying out of his way," he said.

"I wish I could," I said. "The only reason I knew he was in town was because one of the ghosts at the inn came to me earlier, saying his friend disappeared. I looked everywhere, and I couldn't find her."

He arched a brow. "You think he banished one of the town's ghosts?"

"I have no idea," I said. "But I'm naming him as responsible, because he's going out of his way to be obnoxious. He won't say what he's doing in town, but I bet it isn't a simple sightseeing trip. There's nothing to sightsee except for ghosts."

Besides, Reapers rarely did anything without a reason. And if he was here, then the rest of the Reaper Council might well not be far behind.

4

Drew walked me back to the inn after our date, and I did my best to put the Reaper's unwelcome intrusion out of my mind. Somewhere on the way, we'd ended up holding hands, and I could almost forget the haunted streets and my lingering worries about the Reaper's threats to use his spiky instrument against my brother.

When we neared the inn, Drew let go of my hand. "This was a really nice evening."

"It was," I agreed. "If you ignore our unwanted interruption, anyway."

"I'd prefer to do that," he said. "He wasn't very pleasant."

"No, he wasn't." I faced him, my heart racing as he leaned closer.

That, of course, was when my brother decided to float through the door and between us. I jumped back, and Drew frowned. "Your brother?"

"Mart, get out of the way." I waved a hand at him, trying to shoo his ghost aside.

"*That* wasn't nice of you," Mart said. "I thought you'd come running home right away when you heard the Reaper had threatened to use his pointy weapon on me. I'm hurt."

"You knew he was going to interrupt our date?" I said.

"No need to sound so accusing," he said. "You know what he'd have done to me if I'd tried to stop him."

Did I ever. Drew looked at the spot where Mart was floating. "You were following the Reaper. Did you find out where he's staying?"

"Why is he talking to me?" Mart said to me. "He can't even hear me."

"He's trying to be polite, which is more than I can say for some people." My hopes for getting a kiss from the detective had thoroughly evaporated by now. "*Did* you learn anything useful? Like what Shelton's doing in town, for instance?"

"You think I know?" he said. "I managed to follow him for a bit, but he never stopped off at the old Reaper's house. I don't think he's here to see Harold."

"Then I'll pay him a visit tomorrow."

Not that I generally expected much in the way of cooperation from the crotchety old Reaper, but surely the idea of a fellow Reaper in town was worthy of attention, even from him.

"This I'd like to see," said Mart. "I want that guy gone from town as soon as possible. He's trouble."

"I have to agree with you there," I said. "Drew, do you want to come with us and see Harold tomorrow?"

"I think I'll pass," he said. "You aren't going to pick a fight with the newcomer, are you?"

"Not at all." My heart sank when he turned around as though he intended to leave, but the mood was thoroughly ruined, and Mart clearly wasn't going anywhere. "See you soon?"

"Sure," he said. "See you tomorrow."

The moment he was out of earshot, I rotated on my heel. "Thanks, Mart."

"For what?" he said. "I'm not the one who barged into the middle of your date."

At least the Reaper didn't stick around. I bit back the words, more annoyed than I had the right to be. Shelton was the one I was really mad at, anyway.

Whatever he was doing in town, Mart was right. The guy was definitely trouble.

I had trouble sleeping that night. My mind refused to let go of the image of the Reaper swooping around and using his scythe on the local spirits, while Mart was just as restless, frequently floating through the wall connecting my room to the vacant one next door as though reluctant to be alone. Maybe he was afraid of the Reaper showing up, too.

When my alarm went off, I gave up on sleep and decided to make another attempt to track down Lara. When I turned on my Reaper senses, Shelton didn't appear within my sight, so he must have been staying far enough on the other side of town to be out of range. *Good.* I wondered whereabouts he'd chosen to stay, since everywhere in town had its own resident ghosts. Not a single place in town was spirit free.

Despite my best efforts, though, I couldn't find Lara's ghost. Giving up for now, I got dressed and then went downstairs to grab breakfast to go before my visit to old Harold's cottage. Allie beckoned me over to her when I approached the buffet table.

"How was your date?" asked Allie.

"Great," I said, not managing to sound as enthusiastic as I wanted to. In response to her raised eyebrow, I added, "It would have been better if we hadn't been interrupted by the new Reaper in town when he decided to march into the restaurant to be rude to me."

"There's a new Reaper in town?" she asked.

"Yeah, and I'm going to pay a visit to old Harold and ask if he knows the guy and what his deal is." Which was bound to go over as well as a lead broomstick. There was no sense in delaying, though, so I grabbed a piece of toast to eat on the way and set off.

Eric's ghost was floating outside the inn when I walked out. "Hey, Maura."

"Has Lara shown up yet?" I asked.

"No." He raised his head. "Have you seen her?"

"I checked all the ghosts around the inn again this morning, and she's not here," I told him.

"Oh." He shook his head. "I wish I knew where she was."

"Is there anything you haven't told me about the day she vanished?" I asked. "Because I'm actually off to talk to the local Reaper right now, and—"

"You can't tell him!" he said. "We don't need another Reaper coming after us."

"Relax. You know old Harold's retired," I said. "I'm going to talk to him about the new Reaper in town, but it'd help if you could tell me who she might have interacted with before she vanished."

He hesitated, glancing over his shoulder. "We might have annoyed Mrs Terrence the other day."

"How so?" I asked.

The crabby old witch was one of our regular customers and was known for being bad tempered. Getting on her bad side was not a smart move, as our first potential bartender had discovered.

"You know when she was yelling at the kid you were trialling the other day?" she said.

I thought back. "You're the one who moved the plates around?"

"Lara did it," he said. "We thought it was funny. Anyway, that was the day before she vanished."

"Mrs Terrence can't see ghosts, though," I said. "I bet she didn't know it was you."

Or could she? I didn't usually ask people whether they could see ghosts, figuring it wasn't any of my business. Since I was working later that morning, it might be worth asking a few of our regular customers and seeing if they'd witnessed the local spirits' pranks. I might as well try that angle before provoking Shelton again.

In the meantime, though, it was time to see the old Reaper and hope he was a little more cooperative than the new guy. If his attitude to the new arrival was anything like how he'd reacted to me when I'd arrived in town, he might be all too happy to help me get rid of him. Hey, I could dream.

The ghost watched me leave the inn without

following after me. Mart didn't tail me either, but it was probably for the best that he stayed as far from the newcomer as possible. I saw no signs of Shelton on my walk to the cemetery and the cottage sitting at the foot of the hill marked with the number 42. I didn't know if the number had some special significance, since a large proportion of the town's houses were numbered at random anyway, and the Reaper wasn't known for answering questions, so I let Mart keep his theory that Harold was secretly a fan of *The Hitchhiker's Guide to the Galaxy*.

I rapped on the door with my knuckles and waited.

"Go away," said the old Reaper on cue.

"It's me," I said to the closed door. "Have you met the new Reaper who's staying in town? He's called Shelton. Kinda unfriendly."

No answer came for a long moment. Then the door opened a crack, and the old Reaper peeked out. "What are you meddling with this time?"

"Me?" I said. "Nothing. A new Reaper was wandering around near the inn yesterday and wouldn't tell me why he's here. I wondered if he'd come to see you."

"He most certainly did *not*," growled old Harold. "I knew this would happen from the instant you showed up here."

"Excuse me?" I said. "He's not after me. He doesn't seem to care that I'm living in town, in fact. Hence why I assumed he came to visit you instead."

The bloody cheek of it. If Shelton was with the council, he was more likely to be here to target the retired Reaper, who'd been responsible for letting the place end up flooded with ghosts to begin with. All I'd done was a little ghost hunting, which meant I was the less trouble-some of the pair of us.

"Then I hope you'll keep it that way," he said.

"Wait," I said, sensing that he was about to shut the door in my face. "What am I supposed to do if I see him again? Aren't you bothered that he might be banishing your ghosts?"

"He can do whatever he likes," he said. "It's none of my business."

"That's not a helpful attitude to have," I told him. "He might be a rogue, you know."

He grunted. "Then the council can come and deal with him."

"Have you spoken to the council at all since your retirement?" I said. "If they do send someone after him, do you really think they'll let this place stay as it is without reprimanding you for neglecting your duties? You'll have more than a single Reaper on your hands if you continue to ignore him. They won't be pleased with you."

He slammed the door in answer. *Seriously?* The guy was a curmudgeon, but I'd thought he at least cared a little about the town's ghostly inhabitants. More than he did the living, anyway. He ought at least to care about being targeted by the council, right? Maybe he thought if he ignored the problem, it'd leave him alone. Which wasn't a helpful attitude to have.

Shaking my head, I turned my back and retraced my steps to the inn, where I found another of the other local spirits floating around outside.

"Have you seen Lara?" I asked, approaching the young male ghost. "You know, the girl who usually hangs out with Eric?"

"No. Why?" he said.

"She vanished," I explained. "Yesterday, I think. Nobody knows where she is."

"Thought she moved on," he said.

"Not on purpose, if she did," I said. "Eric is worried about her."

"I'll keep an eye out, then," he said.

Had he seen the Reaper? If not, I decided not to bring up the subject. I didn't need to be besieged by terrified ghosts for the whole of my shift, thanks.

I kept myself busy at the restaurant for the rest of the morning, waiting for Mrs Terrence to show up for lunch as she usually did. None of the other customers gave the ghosts a second's glance, and I was starting to doubt there was much point in asking Mrs Terrence, either. Even if the ghosts had been responsible for rearranging her plates the other day, I doubted a harmless prank would have prompted her to take extreme measures, and besides, we'd know if someone had used a banishment charm near the inn. It was hard to keep that kind of thing quiet.

When she came in and took a seat beside the window, setting her grey hat on the chair next to her as though she assumed someone would steal the spare seat otherwise, I made my way over to her table. "Hello, Mrs Terrence. Do you want the usual?"

"What else?" she grumbled.

I kept a pleasant smile firmly in place. "We'd also like to offer you a complimentary drink to make up for the incident during our trial shift other day."

"You aren't hiring that incompetent excuse for a bartender, are you?" she said.

"No, of course not." It didn't sound like she suspected

any spiritual interference, so I did my best to remember her overly complicated order and slipped back behind the bar to make her drink. Unfortunately, my offer seemed to have made her think I was happy to be at her beck and call all afternoon, and she kept calling me over to her table to voice her complaints about everything from the temperature of the room to the lighting.

Thankfully, Allie came to my rescue by calling me back behind the bar. I gladly escaped, and she eyed Mrs Terrence from across the room. "Are you okay?"

"Yeah, I'm just regretting striking up a conversation with Mrs Terrence," I said. "Is she ever happy with anything?"

"No," she said. "What prompted you to offer her a free drink?"

"One of the local ghosts vanished after playing a prank on her," I explained. "You know when she was ranting at that poor kid who was being trialled the other day? I wondered if she knew it was a ghost who was really responsible, so I tried to find out more. That was the only way I could think of to bring up the subject with her."

"Oh." Her expression cleared. "You think she might have sent the ghost away? I doubt she did. She can't see ghosts herself, can she?"

"No, but Lara has been missing for the last two days, and her friend is worried," I said. "I was trying to help him out, but to be honest, I'm more inclined to blame the new Reaper in town for her disappearance."

"Is that why the two of you got off on the wrong foot?" she asked.

"Kind of," I admitted. "My brother followed him in the hopes of finding out where he was staying, but the Reaper caught on to him. So he decided to crash my date with the detective."

"Oh, you mentioned that," she said. "What did he do?"

"Walked into the restaurant and told me to call off my brother or else he'd use his scythe on him," I said. "We're both lucky he at least gave me a warning first."

Her expression darkened. "That's uncalled for. He shouldn't have interrupted your date. Did he know Drew is the chief of police?"

"He does now, but he didn't seem bothered when he found out," I said. "I don't know what his deal is, but I'm glad he isn't staying here at the inn. I bet the ghosts are, too."

"I wonder where he's staying, then," she said. "We're the only inn that is bigger than a small family-run place, and there aren't many others in town anyway."

"I was wondering the same thing," I said. "He said he wanted to stay somewhere he can avoid ghosts, but he's deluding himself if he thinks he'll find a ghost-free haven here in Hawkwood Hollow."

"You're right there," she commented. "With any luck, he'll leave town without any more incidents. You aren't going to speak to him again, are you?"

"No, provided he stays out of my way," I said. "I'd be less suspicious if he actually admitted what he was doing in town, though. I don't know if he works for the Reaper Council, but I can think of several unpleasant things that'll happen if they get wind of how haunted this place is. I want to at least keep an eye on him for that reason."

"I suppose you have good reason to be concerned, then," she said. "If he's going to make trouble, though, the police will see to it that he doesn't step out of line."

"I know they will, but Drew can't see ghosts, nor can the others," I said. "That means it's hard for them to defend the town's dead inhabitants. In fact… I'm probably the only one who can do that, or at least the only person willing to try."

This was a personal issue not just for me but for Carey, whose ghost blog was finally getting some traction. Not to mention we'd spent the last few weeks planning how to turn the inn into a popular haunted tourist destination, which would be kind of difficult with a bunch of angry Reapers running amok in town and chasing all the ghosts away.

Realistically, I'd always known the Reaper Council would notice this place eventually. My own presence in town had stirred things up enough that I understood why old Harold had been reluctant to accept that I'd be staying here. Though he'd somewhat come around to the idea by now, the new Reaper might well wreak a trail of destruction through my new life without even having to deploy his scythe. The guy had an agenda he refused to share, and his barging into the middle of our date yesterday had proved he had no boundaries. But had he really banished an innocent spirit—and what if that was only the beginning?

5

My head remained in the clouds all afternoon, dwelling on the new Reaper and the ghost's disappearance. Carey came into the restaurant while I was cleaning up at the end of my shift, accompanied by Casper. While her familiar bounded onto the table, she sat in her usual seat by the bar, her head down. My heart dropped when I remembered what she'd told me yesterday about the girl in her class who'd started a rival ghost blog. I'd pretty much forgotten, what with everything else going on.

"Hey, Carey," I called to her. "You okay?"

She gave a shrug, and Casper snuggled into her arms, his sad meow answering for her.

"Is it the girl with the blog?" I guessed.

"Cris posted actual ghost footage on her blog last night," she said to me. "And now everyone's sharing it all around school. They're seriously impressed."

"What kind of footage?" I asked.

"Just a few books floating around, that kind of thing,"

she said. "And some creepy rooms in an abandoned old house. Not sure which one."

"You've done better than that," I reminded her.

"Not according to everyone who's read her blog," she mumbled.

"She's popular, right?" I said. "It might not be the ghosts that are the draw if that's the case. You've seen more spirits than anyone else in your class, I bet. That's all that really matters."

"No, it's definitely the ghosts," she said. "She's also set up her own YouTube channel, and she already has over a hundred followers."

"Oh." I didn't know what to say to that. "Carey, I know it's hard, but I wouldn't let it bother you. We can go ghost hunting again this weekend if you like, get some fresh content up there. I know your followers are excited to read more from you."

"She keeps mocking my posts about going ghost hunting with you," she said in a small voice. "She said the only reason I saw any ghosts at all was because I'm friends with a Reaper, and she said it doesn't count."

"Take no notice of her." Easier said than done, I knew. Being fifteen was the absolute worst. I wouldn't have relived my teen years if you'd paid me. "What does it matter if you and I hunt ghosts together? She's probably jealous."

She made an indistinct noise. I hadn't convinced her, but I hadn't expected to either. I wished I had decent advice on hand for dealing with that kind of situation, but the only reason I hadn't suffered worse bullying at school was because everyone had been scared of angering the local Reaper. Unless I grabbed old Harold's scythe and started terrorising her classmates, which Carey probably wouldn't go for. Sure was tempting, though.

A few minutes later, the door opened, and a group of teenagers entered the restaurant. Carey shrank back in her seat, and Casper dropped off her chair, positioning himself protectively in front of her. *Speak of the devil...*

"Is that them?" I lowered my voice, glancing at the newcomers.

She nodded, and Casper let out a low growl, which was surprising coming from such a generally good-natured cat. Like all familiars, he was prepared to defend his witch.

"Which one has the blog, then?" I studied the teenagers. They wore their uniforms from the academy, albeit with embellishments. Most had their skirts hiked up above their knees and were perusing the menu of cocktails they definitely weren't old enough to drink. I followed Carey's gaze to a girl with blond hair who would have been pretty if her face hadn't been plastered with enough fake tan to turn her complexion orange.

That's Cris, is it?

The girls continued looking at the menu without ordering anything, but I didn't miss how they kept glancing in our direction and giggling noticeably. Their whispers seemed to be directed at me as much as at Carey, too. All right, then. If they wanted to issue a challenge, I'd be more than happy to meet them on the battlefield. Scythe or no scythe.

I walked over to their table, ignoring Carey's look of alarm, and halted beside them.

"Can I help you?" I asked. "Are you going to order anything?"

"You're Carey's Reaper friend," said a dark-haired girl sitting next to the blond girl Carey had pointed out. Like Cris, she wore a thick layer of fake tan and another layer of makeup on top of that. If anything, it made her look younger rather than older.

"I'm Maura," I said. "Want me to get you a drink?"

"Sure. I'll have a marshberry whisky," said Cris. "Three of them."

"We don't sell alcoholic drinks to minors."

"I'm eighteen," she insisted.

"Nice try, but I'll have to see some ID," I said. She looked the same age as the others, fifteen or sixteen. "And if you *are* eighteen, you aren't allowed to share those drinks with the others if they're underage."

She muttered something uncomplimentary under her breath, which I dutifully ignored. I definitely did not miss being a teenager. At least as an adult, I had some clout here, though it didn't escape my attention that they all had their wands at the ready, and teenage witches could do some serious damage if they wanted to. Besides, a magical duel in the middle of the restaurant wouldn't improve the situation for any of us.

She reached into her pocket and pulled out an obviously fake ID. I rolled my eyes at the photo on it. "That isn't you. Older sibling, is it? Or an illusion spell?"

Her face reddened under her fake tan. "It's me."

"Uh-huh." She didn't frighten me, though I was curious as to why she'd decided to branch out into ghost hunting, aside from the lure of mocking Carey. She didn't look the type to trek around crumbling old houses on the weekends. "If I were to use a verification spell on this, it'd work, right?"

She took back the ID. "Thought you were a Reaper, not a witch."

"I'm both," I told her. "Pick something else. Go on."

I ignored their mutters, having heard far worse abuse during my few short-lived customer-service jobs. Their bark was worse than their bite. Their assertiveness thinly masked a deep-seated insecurity that was awfully familiar to me, but it irked me beyond belief that they'd chipped away at Carey's self-esteem in their desperate pursuit of gratification.

Allie walked into view, eyeing the group of teenagers. "Everything all right in here?"

"Just perfect," I said without turning around. "Have you picked something else to order?"

"No," said Cris. "We're leaving."

All of them rose to their feet and left in a pack, as though they thought lightning would strike them down if they walked more than a metre apart. I watched them retreat, half prepared for them to turn around and fire a spell at me or something, but they walked out of the restaurant without looking back.

Shaking my head, I returned to Carey's table.

"Is that Cris seriously practising amateur ghost hunting?" I said to Carey. "I can't picture her wandering through an old house, not if she spent as long on her makeup as I think she did."

She gave a shrug. "I don't know what prompted her to start her blog, but she's got enough followers that she's taking it seriously enough to keep talking about it all the time."

"Uh-huh." I shook my head. "She's not that impressive.

I bet she's never been threatened by a terrifying poltergeist or a deranged killer the way you have."

Carey's morose expression didn't lift. "If she takes all the attention away from me, my blog will end up with nobody in town reading it."

"You don't need your classmates to subscribe," I reminded her. "It's more impressive that you have readers who've never met you following your blog and waiting for updates. I bet that Cris doesn't have anyone reading her blog she doesn't already know."

Before Carey could reply, a loud bang came from outside, followed by a series of sparks flying out from somewhere to the side of the door.

"What are they doing out there?" I turned away from the table and headed for the door. Pushing it open, I spotted a couple of uniformed figures running around the corner. Didn't take a genius to know they were up to no good.

"Hey!" I said. "What are you doing?"

The group of schoolgirls halted as one, and Cris rotated on her heel to glare at me.

"Nothing," she said.

Right. "I won't take your word for it on that. If you were using magic to cause damage to the property, I'll have to call the police."

Allie walked out of the inn behind me and approached their group. "What are you doing?"

"Nothing," Cris said, but with less force than before.

"I saw a flash of light from over there," I supplied, indicating their general direction. "What spell were you casting?"

"I didn't cast a spell." Her tone sounded belligerent. "We're not doing anything wrong."

"I'll let you off this once," Allie said, "but I'd advise you to go home before you get yourselves into trouble. Go on, all of you."

She walked back towards the restaurant, while I followed and said in an undertone, "I've got it. I'll make sure they leave."

As she ducked back inside, Carey exited the restaurant behind me, only to halt on the spot when Cris levelled an accusing stare at her.

"You didn't have to set your mother on us," Cris said.

"I didn't," Carey mumbled. "She owns the restaurant. What were you doing out here?"

"Nothing." She pulled out her wand. "Might change my mind if you keep staring at us, though."

"Hey." I stepped in. "You're supposed to be leaving. Unless you want to admit what you were doing, because I'm trying to think of a good reason for you to skulk around here casting spells, and there isn't one."

"We were looking for a ghost," Cris's blond friend blurted.

Well, well.

"Ghost hunting," I said to her. "You can see them, then?"

"What's it to you?" said Cris.

"She's a Reaper, remember?" Her friend eyed me with interest. "You see ghosts."

"I do," I said. "I talk to them, too. Which ghost were you looking for?"

"Ann," hissed Cris. "Quiet."

"You thought there was a ghost here at the inn?" I asked Ann, ignoring Cris.

"Not at the inn," Ann insisted, earning another furious glare from her friend. "Over there by the river."

I followed her gaze down the slope of the riverbank, where it curved around a corner behind the inn. "Tell me about this ghost, then. I'm intrigued."

"Are you going to Reap it?" said Ann. "Where's your scythe?"

"In my room." No need to let on that I didn't have one. If they thought I was hiding a scary weapon in my room, they might be more inclined to stop making trouble for Carey. "Also, I'm not an active Reaper. I don't use my skills against the town's residents, not unless the ghost poses a threat to living people or otherwise needs to be banished for everyone's safety. Most of them don't fit that category. Which ghost were you looking for?"

"We won't tell you." Cris lifted her chin and then glared at her friend as though daring her to speak a word.

"Uh-huh," I said. "Any particular reason?"

Cris's gaze went to Carey. "Because she'll copy our idea, obviously. We got here first."

"We *live* here," I pointed out. "Just saying. If this ghost you're looking for turns out to be a troublemaker, I'll have to deal with it one way or another."

The dark-haired girl fidgeted. I levelled a stare at her, and she blushed. "There used to be an old shack over there by the river. They say two kids from our school died there in the floods. Eric and someone… Lara."

Oh? "Where'd you hear about them, then?"

"At school," said Ann. "There's a plaque in their memory on the wall. We walk past it every day."

"Huh." She'd got the names of the two ghosts right, though I hadn't known they were memorialised at the academy. Not for the first time, I was reminded that Hawkwood Hollow contained more history than it appeared to on the surface, and every ghost had its own story.

But was it a coincidence that one of the ghosts they'd come here to find had disappeared not long ago?

"Anyway, we aren't doing any harm," Cris added. "We're just looking for the ghost, that's all. Nothing else."

Uh-huh. I decided not to let on that the ghost in question had recently vanished, because that would involve mentioning my new feud with the Reaper. I'd rather not have word spreading around the academy of our unwelcome visitor. Besides, with any luck, they'd give up on their ghost-hunting mission once something more interesting came along, and that'd be that.

"You're welcome to have a look around, but if you start causing trouble on our property, then I'll send you packing," I said.

"Why?" said Cris. "Nobody sent Faith Murray away when *she* was nosing around here the other day."

"Who?" I asked.

"A witch," said Ann. "I've seen her here at least once in the last week. She's been all around town."

"Doing what, exactly?" I said.

"She was laying out herbs on the ground," said Cris. "Like some kind of spell."

"Whereabouts was this?" I asked.

"There." Cris jabbed a finger down the path outside the inn, towards the bank of the river. "Nobody came to tell *her* to leave."

"That's because I didn't know she was there," I said, letting scepticism seep into my tone. "Neither did anyone else, either."

"Well, it's true," said Ann. "Anyway, we're leaving now."

Cris looked as though she might argue, then she scowled. "Yes, we are."

"Go on, then." I watched them as they trailed away towards the bridge, making sure they didn't turn around and come back when they thought I wasn't watching them. I'd never heard of this Faith Murray person before, but for all I knew, Cris was lying. She had good reason to want to deflect attention from herself, after all.

As the group vanished onto the bridge, Allie poked her head out of the door. "Are they gone?"

"I think so," responded Carey. "They'll come back, though."

"I'll keep an eye out for them, then." I walked back into the restaurant behind Carey. "I didn't know one of Cris's friends could see ghosts."

"Neither did I." Carey's gaze dropped. "That explains how they got such good footage of that old house yesterday. It was genuine, what Cris posted on her blog. If they were looking for ghosts near the inn, they won't have any trouble finding them."

"Not when the ghost they're looking for has vanished," I said.

"How do you know that?" asked Carey.

"You know those two ghosts whose names they mentioned?" I said. "Cris said they were students at the academy who died in the floods. I guess the place they used to hang out isn't there anymore, so they came to the inn instead. Thing is, I already know one of them disappeared."

"Those kids came here looking for two of our ghosts?" said Allie.

"No," Carey said quickly. "I mean, that isn't why they came here. They probably asked which ghosts were at the inn so they'd have an excuse to come here and make trouble. They don't actually care about the spirits."

"Well, they won't be coming back," said Allie firmly.

"You can't ban them from the whole restaurant," her daughter protested. "If you do, you'll make it worse. I told you that already."

Hands shaking, Carey walked to the table, picked up her schoolbag, and headed for the door connecting the restaurant to the inn's lobby.

"Hang on." I tried to follow her, but Allie shook her head at me. Without stopping, Carey made for the stairs, Casper padding along at her side, until they were out of sight.

Allie and I exchanged glances. "Don't worry about her, Maura. She's just in a rough patch."

"I know," I said. "I wish there was something I can do, but if these kids are messing around with ghosts, this has the potential to get way out of hand. Especially when one of them actually has the gift of seeing them."

The question was, were any of them involved with Lara's ghost's disappearance? I was still inclined to blame the Reaper, but if the students had been searching for stories about local spirits, it might be worth looking into —even if it was just so I'd have another option aside from antagonising Shelton the Reaper again. There were too many unknowns where he was concerned, but until I got him to spill his secrets, I'd get nowhere. On the other hand, Carey would not be impressed with me if I started questioning her classmates to see if any of them had been involved in a ghost banishment.

I'd see what the ghosts themselves said first.

To start off with, I went looking for the teenage ghost again, while Allie returned to the restaurant to deal with the afternoon's customers. It took me a while to find Eric, since he must have gone to hide when the students came in. I circled the entire ground floor of the inn without finding him and was debating sending Mart to hunt him down when I spotted his ghostly figure hovering in the corner of the games room behind the inn's lobby. The room was empty during the day, so I approached him without worrying we might be overheard.

"Hey," I said to him. "Did you know those kids from the academy were looking for you and Lara?"

"No," he said. "Who told them we were here? How'd they even know we existed?"

"Someone at the academy said there's a plaque there with your names on it, so they must have asked for the story," I said. "You sure you didn't know they were looking for you?"

"Of course I didn't know," he said. "They can't see me, can they?"

"Actually… one of them *can* see ghosts," I admitted. "Are you positive you haven't seen any students looking for you and Lara before?"

"I really haven't seen them." He shrank back into the corner. "I just want Lara to come back. Why can't they leave us be?"

I frowned at him. "Can you think of a reason someone would have sent those kids to look for you and Lara?"

He shook his head. "No, I told you. I thought nobody could see us until you came along."

"Except the Reaper," I said, feeling slightly annoyed at the accusing note to his voice. "And the witches and wizards who have the ability to see ghosts, which includes one of those kids."

"They didn't banish Lara, did they?" he asked.

"I have no idea." I opted for the honest approach. "I can't say I know why they would want to, but my list of possible culprits is pretty short. Also, did you see a witch hanging around the other day? The students told me she was laying out herbs in front of the inn, casting some kind of spell. Faith Murray, the kids said she was called."

"No," he said. "I don't know any of these people. I just want to see Lara again."

Without another word, he floated away through the door into the lobby. I didn't blame him for being in a tetchy mood, given the unwelcome news of the academy students' potential ghost-hunting prowess, but it wouldn't kill him to be a little more grateful for my help.

Now that I thought harder, I wondered if he was being totally honest with me. If his and Lara's deaths were widely known throughout the academy, how many other people in town knew his story? Anyone who'd been to the witch academy in the last two decades, potentially, which was a lot of people.

I returned to the restaurant in the hopes of finding Carey, but she was nowhere to be seen. No doubt she'd stayed in her room in the hopes of avoiding her fellow students, and I couldn't say I blamed her in the slightest. I saw her mother working behind the bar and went to talk to her instead.

"Hey," I said. "Allie, have you ever met Faith Murray?"

"Who, the librarian?" she said. "I haven't. Why?"

"The kids from the academy said they saw Faith Murray hanging around the inn, doing some kind of spell," I explained. "They said we ought to have stopped her instead of harassing them instead."

She arched a brow. "Sure they weren't trying to cover up whatever they were doing earlier?"

"No," I admitted. "Seems weird for Cris to throw the blame at some random person who isn't even here, though. They also claimed to be looking for a ghost, who happens to be the same spirit I'm searching for myself, so I'm not convinced that part was a lie."

"Wait, really?" she said. "They were looking for the ghost of a real person, not making it up?"

"They knew the names," I said. "Eric and Lara are a pair of teenage ghosts who haunt the restaurant, but Eric told me Lara went missing a couple of days ago. Now those kids showed up looking for both of them. Call me suspicious, but I reckon there's something dodgy there."

"Who even told them their names?" she remarked.

"Someone at their school," I said. "Their names are on

a plaque in remembrance of the flood victims. Not sure who told them they were ghosts, but apparently their story is well known, and they died somewhere near the inn."

If they'd been following Carey's ghost-hunting exploits, they might have picked up on the notion that the town was swimming in ghosts, even if most of the residents seemed to neither know nor care about their ghostly neighbours. But that didn't explain how those particular ghosts had landed on their radar… nor why one of them had vanished shortly before their visit to the inn.

Allie pursed her lips. "Sounds like their main goal is to make trouble for everyone, especially Carey. I can't say what problem they might have with Faith Murray, though."

"You said she was a librarian?"

"She is," said Allie. "Not at the academy, mind, but if those kids have been pestering her about local spirits, I can see how she might have got irked with them."

"Might be worth talking to her," I said. "Whereabouts is the library? I don't think I've been there before."

"It's on the other side of the river," Allie answered. "You've seen it, I don't doubt. It's opposite the old coven's headquarters."

"Can't forget that place." I suppressed a grimace at the reminder. "I'm not sure Eric is being entirely honest with me about Lara's disappearance, though I'm lost on why he'd hide the truth from me when he's the one who asked for my help. Maybe I'll see if there's any more info at the library."

It was worth a shot, and I wouldn't have minded bringing Carey with me to get her mind off Cris and her fellow witches' ghost-hunting exploits and attempts to belittle her. It wasn't as if we were going to confront a dangerous ghost, and besides, maybe the staff at the town's library could shed some light on the history of the inn's resident spirits.

"Well, it's your choice," she said. "I have to admit I've sometimes wondered how many ghosts we have living among us here and what their stories are."

"It'd be useful to have more details if we're going to turn this place into a haunted hotspot," I agreed. "Did Carey go to her room?"

She nodded. "Carey wants to be left alone, I think. She's had a tough week, and she has to go back to school tomorrow."

"Are you sure you don't need my help in the restaurant?" I asked, reluctant to abandon Carey after the tumultuous day she'd already had.

"No, I'll be fine," she said. "You deserve the night off. Maybe have a second date with the detective."

"Uh-huh." I hadn't actually heard from him since after our first date, something I didn't want to read too much into. I mean, he was busy, and so was I. Besides, I didn't want to draw him into my feud with Carey's classmates, and I was better off looking for information on the ghosts on my own without drawing the attention of our unwelcome new guest in town. "I'll see what he says."

I left the inn once again, heading over the bridge towards the high street, where most of the local witches worked. The shops would be closing up soon, but I pinpointed the library at the far end of the street. As Allie had told me, it stood across from the coven's headquarters, its bricks painted mauve, like most of the town's witch-owned establishments. I hoped that didn't mean the people who worked there had belonged to the coven and had been buddies with Mina Devlin before her departure from town.

I pushed the oak doors open and walked into the library. A middle-aged witch sat behind the counter, dressed in a dusty cloak and a hat decorated with cobwebs, complete with a spider hanging off the end. I wasn't entirely sure whether it was real or decorative. She sure didn't seem like the sort of person who'd be deemed cool enough for a bunch of teens to give the time of day to, much less for them to go to for ghost-hunting tips, but she must have done a convincing job of selling the town's haunted history to them.

"You're the new witch in town, aren't you?" she said. "I've heard about you."

"I'm Maura," I said. "Are you Faith Murray?"

"Ah, no, I'm Debora," she said. "Debora Lowe. History's my specialist area."

"Really?" Curiosity piqued, I walked closer to the desk. "You mean the town's history, or…?"

"I take it you've heard some of the local stories during the time you've spent here in Hawkwood Hollow?" she said.

"You mean the flood?" I said. "Yeah, I have. I actually wanted to learn more about a couple of former students at the academy who died in the floods."

"Oh?" She arched a brow. "Any reason?"

"There's a group of students at the academy who've taken it upon themselves to go hunting for the ghosts of those two spirits," I explained. "Since my friend and I live at the inn and have a ghost blog of our own, we got curious."

"I think I know who you mean," she said. "Those are the kids who came here to the library to badger my colleague with questions, aren't they?"

"You mean Faith Murray?" I said. "Did she have anything to say to them?"

"She assumed they were out to make trouble, and she might not have been wrong," she replied. "Regardless, I decided to humour them. There *were* two students who are known to have died in the floods, and it was quite an odd case at the time, if I remember correctly."

"In what way?"

"The police were never able to rule their deaths an accident," she explained. "The old shack they were hiding in collapsed when the river burst its banks—that much was clear to any witnesses—but there was some evidence of a spell having been used in the area, too. The police never followed up... well, they tried, but there were so many deaths in the floods that the whole case got buried. Intentionally or not."

Whoa. So their deaths might not have been accidental? It wasn't the first rumour I'd heard of a similar incident during the floods. A tragedy like that, unfortunately, could be used to cover up all manner of crimes.

"Didn't the police have any suspicions as to who might have done it?" I asked.

"There was only one suspect at the time," she said. "A classmate of theirs. The kids who came here to the library weren't interested in the actual case, though."

"They were more interested in the ghosts," I surmised.

"They showed up at the inn where I work, which is close to where the two of them died."

"Interesting," she said. "I can't see ghosts myself, but I've always thought of them as pale echoes of the living. I don't know why it didn't cross my mind that we might learn from them, too. And I call myself a historian." She chuckled lightly.

"Uh-huh." I assumed she knew the local Reaper had retired but not that the town was swarming with the dead. I didn't see any ghosts within sight, but no doubt there were more of them lurking farther into the library. "Did you tell those kids anything else?"

"They had no interest in asking me any further questions," she said. "You know… I do have some old newspapers from the time of the floods. I'm sure they have more details on the case. You can borrow them if you take good care of them."

"Oh, sure." I couldn't keep the surprise out of my voice. "Did you not give them to the students?"

"They didn't ask." She turned around and shuffled over to a nearby shelf. "Those young witches can be quite careless, bless them, but I'm sure I can trust you not to damage them. Feel free to borrow the papers for a few days."

"Thanks." I waited by the desk until she returned, carrying a plastic folder containing a few newspaper clippings. She handed them to me, and I carefully transferred them to my shoulder bag. "It's appreciated."

"No problem at all," she said. "I wonder why some stories make it to the surface and others don't. History is biased, of course, but ghosts are capable of speaking for themselves… provided we can hear them."

Some of us hear more than we want to. "Thanks again. It was nice talking to you."

I left the library, my gaze falling on a dark patch on the ground just outside the door. A row of herbs marked its perimeter, and the faint smell of sage drifted through the air.

Sage was one of the few herbs that repelled spirits. That would explain the lack of ghosts. But who had put the herbal barrier around the library—Debora, or Faith Murray? I debated asking, but Faith didn't appear to be around, so I'd have to talk to her another day.

When I returned to the inn, I found no signs of the kids from the academy. Thankfully. Hoping they'd got the message, I had a quick look around to make sure they hadn't left anything behind when they'd been casting spells outside. I didn't see any visible evidence, but there was always the possibility that the students had made up the story about Faith leaving herbs outside the inn.

Before I went inside, I turned on my Reaper powers and scanned the area for any ghosts. The usual suspects registered on my radar, but no Lara. I did see Eric, though, and went to waylay him in the lobby.

"Have you found her yet?" he said.

"No, I haven't." He could try to be a little less impatient, considering I'd volunteered to help him in my own time. "I *did* hear the two of you died when the shack you were hiding in collapsed during the floods. Do you remember?"

The ghost's entire body paled. "Who told you?"

"Debora Lowe at the library," I said. "She had a bunch of newspaper articles from the time of your death, claiming that it wasn't an accident and blaming it on a classmate of yours."

"That isn't—" He broke off. "I don't remember all the details of my death. I *do* remember the floods. Lara and I bunked off school that day, and we were hanging out at an old shack near the river. I remember this kid from school came to yell at us for skiving off. Said we were setting a bad example."

"Ed James, was it?" I'd sneaked a look at the headlines on my walk home.

"That's him," he said. "I remember that, and then… that was it. Everything went blank. Next thing I knew, I woke up like this, and half the town was underwater."

Hmm. Ghosts sometimes blanked out the memory of their death due to trauma or the amnesia that sometimes came hand in hand with being a spirit, especially one who'd been around for a while. But Eric had always struck me as pretty steady as far as ghosts went. He'd remembered Lara, at any rate.

Eric spun around as though startled by something, then he vanished without warning. When I peered through the door, I spotted the detective walking across the bridge towards the inn. He saw me and quickened his pace, and I went out to meet him.

"Hey," he said. "What're you doing alone in the lobby?"

"Talking to a ghost," I said. "Were you on your way here?"

"I was actually looking for you."

"Oh?" My heart gave a flip. "Any reason?"

"For a start, I found out where our Reaper friend is staying," he said.

"You did?" I said. "What ghost-free place did he find in

town? Or is he camping in the nearest field?" He didn't look like the type to enjoy camping, but maybe in his eyes, squatting in a tent in a muddy field was preferable to being pestered by ghosts.

"He's not staying in town," said Drew. "He's at a small bed-and-breakfast place in the village over the hill. I saw him walking there."

My brows rose. "He's staying with the normals."

That would explain a lot, though if he hoped to avoid ghosts that way, he was barking up the wrong tree. Ghosts were just as likely to plague normals as they were paranormals like us if they assumed they could get attention. Besides, he still hadn't confided what he was doing in town, which raised a major red flag in my book.

"Exactly," said the detective. "How's the ghost hunt going?"

"It took an interesting turn," I said. "Let's just say the situation with the teenage ghosts and the academy students is a little more complicated than I thought."

We headed into the restaurant, where Allie gave us a wave from behind the bar. Then I told him about my encounter with Carey's classmates and their strange interest in the ghosts of the two ex-students. I then added that I'd visited the library and confirmed the details of the students' deaths with Debora Lowe, as well as picking up some articles that suggested there might have been more to their deaths than met the eye.

"Those kids were here to make trouble, but I don't know if they were the ones who banished Lara's ghost," I said. "Regardless, it seems weird that one of the ghosts vanished right after a bunch of people started looking for her."

"I thought you were blaming the Reaper for her disappearance," he commented.

"I still think he's the most likely culprit." *I think.* "Not sure how he fits into this, though. He doesn't know the locals, especially victims of a decades-old flood."

"What did you learn from the library, then?" he asked.

"I got these." I reached into my bag and pulled out the folder of newspaper clippings. "Turns out the police weren't clear on whether the two deaths were an accident, and there were a few articles speculating about who did it. I'm guessing it was before your time?"

"It was," he confirmed. "I can check with my colleagues if you think it's relevant to the ghost's disappearance."

"I honestly don't know," I admitted. "The kids from the academy will be annoyed with me if I take their ghost-hunting mission away from them, but I'm not sure Carey wants to put their story on her blog anyway."

"Doesn't she?" he said. "I thought it sounded right up her alley."

"It does, but those kids are *horrible.*" I shook my head. "They came here to rile her up. I'm not sure they even care about the ghosts, but Carey doesn't want to provoke them, so I doubt she'll want to get involved."

Unfortunately, if I took matters into my own hands, they might well take out their annoyance on Carey at school anyway. There seemed to be no way to win in this situation.

"Oh," he said. "Have you spoken to those students yourself?"

"I did, and Carey got mad at me," I said. "Being a teenager is hard enough. I don't need to add to that by intervening with school bullies. I already told them to go away, and they weren't bothered. It doesn't seem like there's a way to win other than to ignore them until they get bored and find someone else to hassle. I know how these things operate."

"You do?" he said. "You didn't have to deal with the same when you were at school, did you?"

I raised a brow. "I wasn't bullied, but I was a Reaper apprentice in a town of witches. My brother was better at playing the role than I was, so he was less of a social outcast than me."

Of course, he'd been alive back then, which had meant I'd always had someone in my corner. That was one reason I'd left town and cut ties with the place I'd grown up in after his death. I'd had no close friends and nobody aside from my family who'd missed me when I left. Man, that was a depressing thought.

Drew's mouth parted. "Your brother's been quiet lately, hasn't he?"

"I think he's lying low after the Reaper told him to go away," I said. "And then there's the missing ghost, too. He probably feels like he's already had one close call and that he's better off not pushing his luck."

"Is he usually that sensible?"

"No, but he hasn't seen a Reaper in as long as I have," I said. "Should we go and pay Shelton a visit now that you know where he's hanging out? Just the two of us, not my brother."

"I don't think he's going to be happy if we corner him at the place he's staying at," Drew said. "Better to wait until we see him in town again, I think."

I pulled a face. "I just wish he'd admit what he's doing here. It'd help if old Harold would cooperate as well. I'd feel a lot easier confronting him if he'd be able to back us up, but he won't even leave that cottage of his."

"Out of curiosity, what happens if it *is* the Reaper who's responsible for the missing ghost?" he asked.

"I have no idea," I said. "If the council sent him, then there's nothing I can do. If he's a rogue, I'm supposed to contact the council myself and inform them so they can swoop in and discipline him, but that's not happening for obvious reasons. So if he turned out to be operating outside of the law, I'd have to take him on directly and drive him out of town myself."

"Is that possible?" he asked. "He has the same abilities that you do, doesn't he?"

"Yeah, which is why I'd rather we didn't come to blows," I said. "He has a scythe. I don't. If I could get old Harold's help, I might be able to drive him off, but on my own, I'm more likely to end up coming off worse."

"Maybe he'll respond if the police confront him," he said. "I don't think we've ever arrested a Reaper before, but we have the resources at our disposal to make sure he doesn't get away with any crimes."

I pressed my mouth together. "Not that I don't appreciate it, but if it goes on official records, word might make it back to the Reaper Council anyway."

And then? The new life I'd begun to build since my arrival in town would potentially be in danger. I'd been under no illusions that I might be able to keep my history at bay forever, but I'd started to act as if that was the case all the same. And while I didn't like to admit it, it was easier to pretend the other Reapers didn't exist. After all, acknowledging them meant facing the people who'd indirectly caused my brother's death and generally screwed up my life.

"All right," he said. "I'll keep it quiet for now unless you change your mind. I need to head back to the pack territory for an event tonight, but I'll come and talk to the Reaper with you tomorrow."

"What event?" I folded my arms, keeping a teasing tone. "Am I not invited?"

"A pack thing," he said. "Like the coven's social events but with werewolves instead of witches."

"Ugh."

"I thought that'd be your reaction." He grinned. "I would like to see you again, though, just in case I wasn't clear on that one. We can go out another night."

My heart gave another skip. "Sure. That sounds good."

"You don't sound all that enthused," he remarked.

"I've had a trying day," I said. "Carey's already mad at me because of the thing with her classmates."

"I'm sure she isn't," he said. "Maybe go and talk to her?"

"If she'll let me." I rose to my feet and walked with him to the door. "See you tomorrow?"

"Sure." He waved goodbye to me as well as to Allie, who was watching from behind the bar, and left the restaurant.

As for me, I would have stayed downstairs to grab something to eat, but Carey was notably absent, and I hadn't checked on Mart, either. I headed up to my room, hoping he wasn't freaking out too badly because of the missing ghost. My room was empty, but the instant I called his name, he appeared.

"There you are," he said. "Aren't you going on a date with the detective?"

"He's busy tonight," I said. "Pack thing. No, you can't go and crash the party. Anyway, I have an update on our ghost."

I told him about my encounter with the academy students and then my visit to Debora Lowe and the articles she'd given me on Lara's and Eric's deaths.

"You're saying she's the one who sent those students here?" he said.

"Nah, they came here of their own accord," I said. "I think they were more interested in bothering Carey than ghost hunting, so I sent them packing."

"They'd better not come back," he said. "If they do, I'll chase them off myself."

"You're welcome to chase them out of the inn if they do anything else to Carey," I said. "But she doesn't want us interfering on her behalf, so I have another idea."

"Oh, boy," he said. "No, I am *not* following that Reaper again."

"You didn't think I'd ask you to risk your neck, did you?" I said. "No, it's not about that. Carey is pretty upset over those kids picking on her, and I don't think I helped the situation much."

"No, you didn't," he said.

"Thanks," I said. "I wondered if you wanted to help me cheer her up. I was going to grab some food from downstairs and put a movie on, and you can play some ghostly tricks for her camera."

He rolled his eyes. "I'm not a performance artist."

"I'm not asking you to do it for an audience," I said. "Just Carey, who might end up quitting her ghost-hunting blog if those kids keep interfering, and then you won't be able to show off for the cameras at all. Besides, I thought it would be more fun for you to watch a movie with us rather than hanging around on your own."

"All right," he said. "Can I pick the movie?"

"I'll see what Carey says," I said. "Look, just… try to be nice. I know Carey can't hear you, but I can, and she can read my face. I don't want her coming out of this feeling even worse than she did already."

"I'll be on my best behaviour," he promised.

Mart followed me out of the room and down the corridor to the suite where Carey and her mother lived. I knocked on the door, but Carey didn't answer.

Without preamble, Mart floated through the door's wooden surface and into the room.

"Mart, don't do that," I said to the door. "Come on, at least wait to be invited in first."

The sounds of footsteps came from inside the room, and Carey's muffled voice sounded behind the door. "Is your brother in here?"

"He came to cheer you up," I answered. "I forgot he can't follow instructions."

Carey opened the door, her eyes slightly red. "Where is he now?"

I peered over her shoulder into the living room of her shared suite. The door to her bedroom lay open at the back. Her room had papers scattered all over the floor, along with her ghost goggles and several other half-built contraptions. Casper was curled up on her bed, snoozing, while Mart danced around in the background.

"He's doing the Macarena, I think," I said. "He's a terrible dancer."

"You're worse," Mart retaliated.

A smile tugged at her mouth. "He came to see me?"

"Sure," I said. "We wanted to know if you'd be up for watching a movie tonight. I'll grab some food from downstairs first, and the three of us can watch something fun. Sounds good?"

"I thought you were going out with the detective," she said.

"He's busy tonight," I said. "Pack thing."

"That's a shame," she said. "I thought you two were hitting it off. You had a nice first date, didn't you?"

"We did." I sought a change of subject before Mart started making unwanted comments about Drew again. "We're planning on another date soon, but we're both busy."

"Or running away," Mart said. "You always do this. You have one good date with a guy, and then you get cold feet and run off."

I shot him a glare, which he ignored. "We're doing something this weekend, I think, assuming our grumpy Reaper friend doesn't barge in on us this time."

"Old Harold interrupted your date?" said Carey.

Ack. This was why I didn't get people involved in my personal life. It complicated everything. It'd also slipped my mind that I hadn't updated her on the new Reaper situation. "Not Harold. There's another Reaper visiting town, and he isn't my biggest fan."

"Why?" she said. "Who is he?"

"He got annoyed because I sent my brother to spy on him to figure out what he was doing here," I explained. "Honestly, I'm still not sure what he's doing here, but Mart's not taking the risk and spying on him again."

"I should bloody well hope not," said Mart. "His threats took ten years off my afterlife."

"Why were you interested in where the Reaper is staying?" asked Carey.

"We don't think he's supposed to be here," I said, opting for an honest approach. "We also think he might have banished one of the two ghosts Cris and her friends were looking for."

She paled. "What? You're looking for them, too?"

"No, but I already spoke to Eric a few times this week," I said. "He's worried because Lara disappeared. I think the Reaper is to blame, but the guy's being cagey about why he's really in town."

Her expression cleared. "You think another Reaper is attacking the town's ghosts?"

"I hope he isn't, but he's the most likely culprit," I said. "I think Lara might have been targeted by accident, but it seems weird that her name came up again. I didn't realise she and Eric were students at the academy."

"I don't know anything about them," she said. "I didn't even know the names of the ghosts Cris and her friends were searching for here."

"If she was telling the truth." Glad we'd steered the topic away from the detective, I got out the plastic folder of articles Debora Lowe had given me. "Granted, Eric himself might have hidden some of the details about his death, according to these articles."'

She looked at them in puzzlement. "Where'd you get those?"

"The library," I said. "Debora Lowe gave them to me."

She winced. "You went to the library?"

"Yeah, I did," I said. "I wanted to see if there was

anything else I needed to consider if I'm to find Lara's missing spirit. Want to look at them?"

"I can't read those," she said quietly. "If I do, Cris and the others will think I'm investigating their ghost for my blog. They'll make me stop."

"You don't have to read them," I said, "but if they try anything more, then I'll make it clear that they'll have to go through me if they have an issue with what you decide to write on your blog."

"Don't," she said. "It'll make things worse."

She was probably right. I'd been intending to drive Mart's attention away from the detective by bringing it up, but I hadn't meant to upset her again in the process.

"I'll chase them off," said Mart. "Maybe give one of them a push into the river…"

He would, too, but we'd have to tread carefully when it came to those students. I didn't think they were the ones who'd banished the ghost—and her death had occurred before most of them had been born—but they were drawing my suspicions all the same.

"If you really don't want us to, then I won't show you articles," I said to Carey. "I doubt the students have met the Reaper, anyway. It's him I'm interested in, not them. I won't say a word to them."

"Thanks, Maura," she said.

"Hey, I'm not going to make anyone's life harder than it already is," I said. "Living or dead."

As for the ghosts? They'd have to wait for our movie night to be over before pestering me again.

7

The following morning, I gave a quick read of the articles Debora had given me, since Carey had flat-out refused to get involved. I didn't blame her for that, but the articles themselves were less helpful than I'd hoped. They mostly consisted of rumour and speculation about the two teenagers' deaths, littered with claims from their grieving parents that they hadn't been skiving off school and had been set up.

"This sounds downright accusatory, to tell you the truth," I remarked to Mart. "Like they wanted to blame someone."

"As opposed to admitting their own kids were making out in a shed when the town was flooding?" Mart said. "Nah, I reckon it was a tragic accident."

"Maybe." I flipped to the next article. I wasn't supposed to be working that morning, but I'd woken up early, and Carey was already at school, giving me little else to do with my time. "But there was something odd about Eric's account of his death. He doesn't remember much of it."

"Which is unusual… how?" he said. "I don't like thinking about *my* death either."

"He doesn't even remember the flood, though." I shook my head. "If he was telling the truth, that is. It's not like I can ask Lara to confirm his story."

"Because she's gone," said Mart. "Please tell me you're not going to provoke that Reaper again."

"I'm not going to provoke him. I'm going to ask a few pointed questions about his reasons for being in town." I put the articles aside. "I don't think I'm going to get any useful information out of these, anyway. The detective and I are going to track down our elusive Reaper later."

Mart scoffed. "I swear, if he Reaps my soul, I'll send every ghost in the afterlife to haunt you."

Then he floated through the wall to his room and disappeared.

"No need to be dramatic," I said to the wall, but he didn't return.

Rolling my eyes, I headed downstairs. After breakfast, I took it upon myself to do some cleaning and other chores in the restaurant despite Allie's objections. It wasn't like I had much else to do with my time, since Mart had taken my comments about the ghost banishment to heart and refused to come out of his room. Anyway, cleaning gave my mind space to wander and think more about the articles I'd borrowed from the library while I waited for Drew to show up. He'd promised to visit old Harold with me, but despite that unappealing prospect, my heart lifted when the detective walked into the restaurant. "Hey, Maura."

"Good, you're here," said Allie, interrupting my own greeting. "Take her away before she starts sweeping the floors, too. Not being able to find a replacement bartender doesn't mean you have to do everything yourself, Maura."

"Maybe not, but I'd rather sweep the floors than visit the Reaper," I said. "Is that the plan, Drew?"

"If you mean old Harold, he refused to even open the door to me when I dropped by this morning," he said. "But I do have more information on those two teenage ghosts, too."

"Oh?" I joined him, waving goodbye to Allie as we left the restaurant. "What do you have?"

"I found the case files for those two students' deaths," he said. "Things were so chaotic at the time that a lot of files got misplaced, so there isn't much information available."

"I read over the newspaper articles Debora gave me," I said. "There wasn't much in there, either. It looks like their parents didn't want the whole world knowing their kids were skipping school when they died, so they tried to pin the blame on the last person who saw them alive. In fairness, it also seemed like the newspapers were fishing for a story to be sensational for the sake of it."

"You know the basics already, then," he said. "I don't think there's much more in the police reports except for one suspect who was questioned and then released without being charged with anything."

"Same guy mentioned in the articles, by any chance?" I said. "Is he still around these days?"

"Ed James," he said. "He's living here in Hawkwood Hollow, but he'll be in his thirties now, I think. He and the victims were classmates. I have his address, so we can pay him a visit."

"You want to go and talk to him now?" I asked.

"Sure, if you're up for it," he said. "I'm off duty, technically speaking. Can't have everyone thinking I opened up an old case."

"Better not let word get back to those academy kids, then. Otherwise they'll think we're probing into the town's history to stop them from going ghost hunting," I said.

He raised a brow. "Aren't most of them fifteen? They weren't even born when the floods took place."

"You don't know how mean teenage girls can be, do you?"

"I have an inkling," he said. "I know Carey doesn't want us to intervene, but I'm not certain that ignoring the problem will make it disappear."

"Yeah," I said. "She doesn't have any friends her own age, and I'm starting to think those kids are the reason. They're screwing with her confidence in a major way, and now she's finally started making headway with this ghost blog thing, and they're trying to sabotage that, too."

"You're saying this Debora Lowe from the library is the one who told the students where the ghosts were hiding?" he said.

"No, but Cris and her friends figured out that Eric and Lara were hiding in a shack near the inn when they died, so they decided to come there to bother Carey," I said. "Debora said they weren't that interested in the details of the actual deaths, so she gave me the articles rather than handing them over to those students."

"The police department was frankly a mess at the time," Drew said. "I'm not supposed to say that, but they were inefficient and completely ill-equipped to deal with a situation as serious as the floods. They were also used to stepping aside and letting the coven leader do as she wanted. I gather she had a fair bit of input when it came to the response to incidents like that."

"You mean she might've doctored the newspapers' focus?" I'd already disliked Mina Devlin enough already, but pinning a double murder on a stranger struck me as exactly the kind of thing she'd do. She'd certainly covered up a fair number of crimes during her tenure as coven leader during the short time I'd been in town. "I don't know this Ed James, but with all the ghosts around, the truth was bound to come to the surface eventually. Whether he did it or not."

Since the town hadn't been flooded with ghosts before the Reaper's retirement, I could understand why people might've thought they could get away with murder, but now, not so much. Had the case resurfaced because someone had wanted to get rid of the evidence by any means possible, even this long after the crime had been committed? And how did the other Reaper connect to a long-ago crime that had never been solved? The two seemed to have nothing to do with one another —unless this wasn't Shelton's first visit to Hawkwood Hollow.

"Want to come and speak to him now, then?" he said. "You can tell Carey if you like, but I'm not sure she'll be keen on the idea."

"She won't mind us speaking to him as long as we don't let anything slip in front of those other kids," I said. "They shouldn't come back to the inn if they're sensible, though. Anyway, I'd like to hear what Ed James has to say."

We left the inn and headed over the bridge towards the high street.

"How's work going?" Drew asked.

"Not too bad," I said. "We might need to put out another ad if we don't find another bartender soon. It really shouldn't be this difficult to find someone."

I couldn't help wondering if someone had been spreading stories about us outside of the coven as well, because we hadn't had any applications from non-witches and -wizards either. That or the fact that Hayley had been a murderer had put most people off applying, which was a possibility.

"I did ask some of the pack members last night," he said. "You might get some interest there."

"Oh, thanks," I said. "It's appreciated."

"We're almost there." He led the way down one of the cul-de-sacs in the witches' area of town. "How much do you want to tell Ed James about why the case has come to the surface again?"

"I think I should avoid mentioning that Lara's ghost has gone missing," I said. "If he *did* murder both teenagers, then the best way to get a confession is to pretend the ghosts and I have been chatting with one another."

"Unless he knows the ghost is gone already, even if he didn't do it," he said. "Not that I'm supposed to jump to conclusions, mind."

"I'm more interested to hear what he has to say about Mina Devlin," I added. "I wonder how much input she had in him taking the blame for their deaths."

Drew led the way to a terraced house and knocked on the door. A tall guy with thinning dark hair, presumably Ed James, answered.

"Detective Drew Gardener, right?" he said, blinking in surprise. "Can I help you with something?"

"Yes," said Drew. "If it's okay with you, I'd like to ask you a couple of questions about an incident a few years ago involving the deaths of two of your classmates at the local academy."

The colour drained from his face. "Lara and Eric, right?"

"That's right," said Drew.

"Why are you bringing this up now?" he asked. "I was sad they died, but it's been twenty-odd years."

"Because their ghosts have been haunting the inn ever since then," I said. "I've spoken to them myself, in fact."

Ed visibly blanched. "What did they say?"

"For a start, Eric claimed you cornered him and Lara behind the river when you were supposed to be at school and told them off for skiving."

He shook his head. "I didn't corner them. I was a prefect at the academy, so I was supposed to set a good example. I told them to go back to school, that's all."

"And...?" I said with a significant look at him.

"And what?"

"That's the last thing Eric said he remembered before his death," I said. "He doesn't recall anything else. Not even the flood."

"Maybe his memory is faulty," Ed said. "After I told the pair of them off, I went back to school. News reached the academy that the town was flooding a few hours later, and I didn't know they still were by the river at the time."

"I understand that you were the main suspect," Drew told him. "The police brought you in for questioning."

"Only because I saw them bunking off school. We

were classmates, and we didn't get along, but I didn't do anything to either of them. I thought they drowned."

Hmm. It seemed Eric had gaps in his memory, unless he'd omitted details on purpose. Or was he just shaken to have been reminded of an old, unpleasant part of his own history? It was impossible to tell, especially with a ghost.

"They didn't blame you directly," I said carefully. "But you were the only suspect listed in the police's records. Are you sure you have nothing else to say about their deaths that you didn't tell the police at the time?"

"Of course not," he said. "I—I can't believe they've been here in town all this time. I really didn't know."

"Actually, there's a lot of ghosts in Hawkwood Hollow," I said. "Since the floods, there've been dozens of them in the area. Eric and Lara aren't that unusual."

He looked even more shaken than before. "Right. Good to know. Um, is there anything else? Because I really don't know anything more."

"Did you know Mina Devlin?" I asked.

"Who, the coven leader?" he asked. "You're the one who ran her out of town, right?"

Did everyone in the entire town know? No wonder we'd had so much trouble finding anyone to work at the inn. "I'm the one who exposed the crime she helped cover up, yes. She was the coven leader at the time of the floods, too, wasn't she?"

"I think so, but I wasn't part of the coven, and I didn't know her," he said. "Is that all?"

Hmm. He didn't seem to know anything about the coven leader, but if she'd helped him cover up a crime, then he might be lying to save face. Unless she'd merely pinned the murder on him because he'd been a convenient scapegoat. I wouldn't have put anything past her.

"If we have any other questions, we'll let you know," Drew added. "Thanks for speaking to us."

As Ed closed the door, Drew and I left the house behind us and walked down the street until we were out of earshot.

"What do you reckon?" I asked him. "He seemed pretty surprised that you mentioned the murders at all, though I guess anyone would be if they didn't know how many ghosts were hiding under their feet. Especially people he knew when he was a kid. Do you think he was telling the truth?"

"I'm inclined to think he was," he said. "If he did leave the area hours before their deaths, the details of his whereabouts ought to be easy to check, and from what you told me about the reports, it does sound like the coven wanted someone to blame."

"Mina Devlin strikes again." I rolled my eyes. "I guess they couldn't properly investigate until the floods were cleared up, by which point the perpetrator might have hidden the evidence, if there was any."

"Exactly," he said. "Whether Eric and Lara's deaths were accidental or not, Lara's ghost's disappearance might not necessarily be connected with the way she died or who killed her."

"Not if the Reaper's the one who banished her," I said. "I doubt *he* had anything to do with the case. Even if he was an active Reaper at the time, old Harold was actively dealing with the town's ghosts up until he lost his apprentice. He wouldn't have let another Reaper run amok around here. Besides, it makes no sense for him to come back here twenty years after their deaths."

Which meant there was a good chance the Reaper had another reason for being in town.

"You're right," he said. "Want to go back to the inn, or should we pay the new Reaper a visit? Up to you."

"Yes," I said. "To the second one, I mean. I can't think of anyone else to ask about missing ghosts. If we can figure out what he's doing in town, we might be able to strike him off the suspect list."

Or elevate him to the top. One way or another, it was past time for us to pin Shelton down and get some real answers about what he was doing here. I was done giving him the benefit of the doubt.

It'd have been easier for me to fly to the next town on a broomstick rather than walking, but it was a nice day, and I didn't mind spending some more time with the detective. We chatted as we walked, free from any eaves-droppers. Mart wasn't around either, but that was to be expected. He'd be better off staying far away from our grumpy Reaper friend in case he got mad at Drew and me for cornering him and pulled out his scythe.

The neighbouring town turned out to be even smaller than Hawkwood Hollow, consisting of a single cobbled high street and not much else. It felt strange walking among normals after spending the past few weeks entrenched in the paranormal world. While both Drew and I looked ordi-nary enough most of the time, I had to remember to keep my wand hidden in my pocket. My Reaper side wasn't visible to most people anyway, so I'd just have to remember not to strike up a conversation with any ghosts.

We approached the bed-and-breakfast Drew had located, a pleasant brick cottage decorated with curtains of ivy, and walked in. A woman sat behind the desk, plainly dressed in comparison to the magical folk I'd grown accustomed to spending the majority of my time around over the last few weeks.

"Hey there," said Drew. "We're here to speak to one of your guests. He'd have arrived here a couple of days ago. Shelton…" He looked to me as though it'd just occurred to him that I hadn't mentioned whether Shelton was his first name or surname. With a Reaper, it was lucky we'd got any name from him at all.

"He's gone," the woman answered. "Went out a few hours ago."

"What do you mean, he's not here?" I said. "Will he be staying here tonight, too?"

The woman looked uncomfortable. "Do you know him? Why do you want to find him?"

I hadn't expected it to be easy to find the Reaper, but it looked like we'd come all this way for no reason. Either he'd seen us coming and given us the slip, or he'd gone back into town to do some more poking around. Or worse… ghost hunting.

"No worries," said Drew, sidestepping her questions. "Thank you for your help."

As soon as Drew had closed the door behind us, I said, "Does she know you're the chief of police in Hawkwood Hollow?"

"Probably not," he said. "We do work with the local authorities when appropriate, but we don't tend to mingle with normals."

"Yeah, that's pretty typical of a paranormal community," I said. "The Reaper must have his reasons for picking this place to stay. Aside from not wanting ghosts to bother him, that is."

I assumed he'd booked the trip in advance, so he hadn't seemed to even consider the Riverside Inn as a potential option. Maybe because he'd already known he didn't want to stay inside the town itself... or maybe because he'd had an issue with the place even before he'd known there was a Reaper working there.

Had he known? I wouldn't have thought word would have spread outside the town, but something about the way everyone seemed to be avoiding the inn rubbed me up the wrong way. Even someone like him, who wasn't from Hawkwood Hollow at all and shouldn't know anything about recent events.

Drew studied the cobbled street in front of us. "Want to wait here for Shelton to come back? He can't stay out all day, and I'm inclined to think he'll be returning to stay the night."

"Nah, he's not worth sticking around for," I said. "Let's go back to Hawkwood Hollow. Maybe he's hanging around at the inn again."

I hoped *not*. Especially with both of us absent at the same time. It wasn't as if I had someone else watching out for ghost-related trouble... except for Mart, that is, and I didn't want *him* going near the Reaper again if I could help it.

We headed back along the woodland trail connecting the town to Hawkwood Hollow. It was easy to tell when we were back in town when the number of ghosts multiplied, which at least confirmed that they were localised in that area in particular. Old Harold had certainly left a huge mess to clean up. If the Reaper Council ever decided to make the town its target, they'd need to send more than a lone Reaper to deal with it.

I wasn't sure that was what was going on here, though. One Reaper couldn't expel the ghosts of an entire town, true, but was there a reason he'd picked that ghost in particular to send to the afterlife? If so, then perhaps there was some unknown link between him and the case. Or, if he was a rogue, perhaps someone who *was* involved had hired him to use his scythe to take the ghost out of the picture.

Neither option signalled anything good.

8

Drew and I returned to the inn without running into Shelton on the way back, though not for lack of trying. At least I knew the way to the neighbouring village now if I ever needed to go there again in the future. I'd mostly kept to myself in other towns I'd lived in, and Hawkwood Hollow was more confusing than most due to the bizarre street numbering system, but the route around the town was starting to stick in my memory now I'd walked around so much.

The more I looked out for our missing Reaper, though, the more frustrated I grew. There were a limited number of places he might be hiding, since there was nothing else in the area except for empty fields. The number of ghosts who appeared on our way back into the town signalled that he hadn't gone on a banishing spree, at least, but I was pretty sure the guy hadn't gone to hang out with the witches at the Crooked Broomstick or to a pack party with the local shifters. I doubted he had a single friend in the entire town.

When we passed by the high street, I veered sideways into the road leading to the cemetery on the off chance that Shelton had decided to visit the old Reaper's cottage while we'd been gone. You never knew.

"Want to knock?" asked Drew when I pressed my ear to the door to see if I could hear voices inside.

"Nah, better not risk it." I backed away from the door to old Harold's cottage in case he heard us outside and came out to yell at us to go away. "I don't think our new Reaper friend is in there, besides."

Not that I'd expected him to be, but this game of cat and mouse was getting old.

I was more than happy to go back to the inn and chill out for the rest of the day, but the universe had other plans. After we crossed the bridge, Mart accosted me at the door to the inn. "There's trouble."

"Trouble?" I said. "Like what?"

The detective paused behind me. "Is that your brother?"

"Yes. He says there's trouble at the inn." I turned back to face Mart. "What is it?"

"If you'll let me speak," he said, "I'd tell you. The ghosts are getting seriously agitated in there."

"Including Eric?" I asked.

"He's gone," said Mart. "Allegedly, he disappeared not long after you left. I was in my room, minding my own business, so I didn't see, but I heard the other ghosts calling for him, and they couldn't find him. They searched the whole inn, and the grounds, too."

"Eric has gone, too?" Damn. I shouldn't have turned my back on him, but I'd been at a loss as to how else to find the Reaper. *Did Shelton banish them both?*

"According to Pam here," said Mart. "Come and speak to her."

"All right." I walked into the inn, where another teenage ghost hovered in the corner of the lobby, her eyes big and frightened. "Hey. Mart said Eric's ghost is gone?"

"He's disappeared," said Pam. "He went outside a couple of hours ago, and I haven't seen him since."

"Did he say where he was going?" I asked.

"No, but he was looking for Lara," she said. "That's all he's been doing for the last couple of days. He misses her."

"I know he does," I said. "He asked me to find her. Now he's gone missing, too, apparently. Did you see anyone else outside—anyone living, that is?"

"I didn't leave the inn," she said. "Please, Reaper. Protect us."

"I'll try to." Not that I'd done a spectacular job so far. One ghost's disappearance was bad enough, but two? More to the point, both had disappeared outside the inn, suggesting the person who'd banished them had come here for that very purpose, Reaper or not.

Drew looked at me. "Both ghosts have disappeared?"

"Looks that way," I said. "I don't know when it happened, but if it was a witch who did it, maybe they left some traces behind this time."

It was a long shot, I had to admit, but I was starting to wish I'd never left the inn to begin with. Not only had our trip to visit Ed James proven fruitless, but our unwanted guest had gone walkabout as well. I assumed Allie had more sense than to let him into the inn, but the dude could walk through walls if he wanted to.

Still, so could I. I turned back to face Mart. "Sure you

didn't see anyone come in, through the door or otherwise?"

"Positive," he said. "I *am* a Reaper, you know."

"Okay," I said. "I'm going to search outside."

"I'll go with you," said Drew. "Just in case you try to jump into the river again."

"Hey, that wasn't deliberate," I protested at his reference to an incident a few weeks ago when I'd gone out to do a little solo investigating into a murder case and nearly got myself shoved into the river by the killer. "Anyway, I'm not going that close to the river this time."

"Bet he wouldn't object to having to fish you out." Mart snickered. "He just wants an excuse to get up close and snuggly with you."

I ignored him, walking out in front of the inn. "Stand back. I'm going to check for our Reaper first. Hopefully, he won't notice."

"What do you mean by check?" Drew said.

"Like this." Shadows spread out from my feet, though I made sure not to let them touch the detective. "If I look through the afterworld, I'll be able to see if he's hiding in the building. I can detect his location if he's nearby, too."

Drew's response went unheard as the shadows thickened, revealing the glowing light of several ghosts... and no Reaper. He might still be in town but not within reach of my Reaper senses unless I extended them farther, and I preferred not to smother the entire inn in shadows.

Instead, I let the shadows drop. Drew stood inches from my face, concern pulling at his mouth. "I'm not going to pretend that wasn't unnerving, Maura. It's like you vanished into the shadows."

"Still here." I poked him in the arm to prove my point.

"Our Reaper, though… he isn't here. Neither are our missing ghosts. Maybe they eloped together, but can ghosts even do that?"

"You're the expert," said Drew lightly.

"Not really." I'd never felt more lost, to be honest. "Right. I've searched the afterworld, so all that's left to do is to search the physical world."

"Who's getting physical?" Mart said, floating through the door behind us.

"Nobody," I said. "I told you, I'm searching the area for the missing ghost. Coming to help?"

"No, thanks," he said. "If there's a ghost-eating pit hidden outside, I'm not falling into it."

"There's no such thing as a ghost-eating pit, Mart." I rolled my eyes. "Also, don't say that in front of the other ghosts, please. I don't need them panicking even more."

"What exactly are we looking for?" asked Drew. "Clues that point to a ghost being banished? I know there's a few herbs that'll do the job."

"You've been researching," I observed. "Yeah, there's a few variants. Also, sage is a ghost repellent. That might have been used if they wanted to drive a ghost out of a certain area. Some other herbs will do the trick as well."

Drew and I walked around the inn, scanning the ground for any signs of a banishment spell. Other than mud churned up from the overnight rain and the persistently flowing river, we found nothing. I did another check on the afterworld closer to the river, but I saw neither of the spirits we were looking for, nor the Reaper.

"Nothing?" said Drew.

"Not so far." I banished the shadows again. "Either Eric

wandered out of his usual zone and is hiding elsewhere in town, or…"

Or the Reaper had used his scythe on him and then vanished into the shadows before we returned to the inn.

I spotted Allie watching us from the window of the restaurant and walked back to meet her. "What are you and the detective doing out there?"

"Another ghost is gone," I said. "Eric disappeared while we were out searching for our elusive Reaper."

Her eyes rounded. "You mean the teenager who was looking for the other missing ghost?"

"Looks like he did a runner or was banished," I said. "Who else has been at the inn since we left?"

"The usual lunch crowd," she said. "Not many people. Mrs Terrence… a few others."

"Not those students?"

She shook her head. "I'd definitely know if *they* were around. Besides, they're at school."

"Typical." I released a sigh. "I mean, it's possible he did a runner and went looking for Lara's ghost elsewhere in town, but I don't know. Seems fishy to me that they both vanished within the space of a few days."

"Did you and Drew go to speak to the Reaper, then?" she asked.

"We didn't find him," I said. "He wasn't at the accommodation where he was renting a room, and we walked all over the town and didn't find him. Hence why he's still on my suspect list."

Mart scoffed. "If you ask me, he saw you coming and ran off."

I frowned at my brother. "He's not at the place he's supposed to be staying at, which means he must be somewhere in town. It's not like we're in a big city, so he must have tried pretty hard to hide himself."

"Not necessarily," said Drew. "He might be visiting a friend…"

"A friend?" I snorted. "You think he has friends? If he wasn't visiting the Reaper, I can't think who else he'd speak to. We don't exactly have a ton of tourist attractions."

The ghosts were the town's only feature, but given Shelton's earlier remarks about wanting to stay away from the spirits altogether, I doubted any of the local ghosts were friendly with him even if he *hadn't* been responsible for banishing any of them. He'd have no more friends among the dead than among the living.

"Fair point," said Drew. "I need to head back to the office and put away those case files before someone asks why I got them out."

"Yeah. I might look over the clippings Debora gave me again," I said. "I'm not sure Ed James was guilty of their deaths, but it's weird how both their spirits disappeared in the space of a week, and it doesn't seem to be linked to how they died."

Not if the Reaper was the culprit. For all I knew, though, other local spirits were disappearing, unnoticed by any of the living. Not a pleasant thought at all.

After Drew had left the inn, I headed up to my room, mostly to get some privacy to think and to decide whether to make a monumentally huge gamble. Shelton plainly did not want to be found. Whether that made him guilty was a mystery, but I wasn't about to wait one more day and potentially let him go on another ghost-banishing spree.

I had one way to find him, which Drew would *not* approve of, but I also wouldn't be able to bring him along for the ride. Okay, theoretically, I could, but if it went wrong, Drew was the one who'd likely come off worse. Very little could hurt a Reaper, but a human, even someone as capable as him, was likely to end up in some serious trouble if Shelton was working against the law. Then again, the one thing that *could* hurt a Reaper was another Reaper. Even a half Reaper like me.

Mart interrupted my contemplation by floating through the wall. "What are you doing in here?"

"Deciding whether to take a massive risk or not," I said.

"You're going out with the detective again?" he asked.

"Nope, I'm tracking our Reaper friend using a method I haven't tried yet."

He whistled. "You haven't done that in a while."

"If I do, he won't be able to run or hide from me. He might get on the defensive." On the plus side, I'd be able to pull out all the stops against him. On the minus side? It might get ugly.

Challenge accepted, then.

Once again, I used my Reaper skills and tuned in to the afterlife. Shadows flooded the world, blanking out everything else, and the inn disappeared along with everyone inside it. But instead of searching for ghosts, I scanned for the familiar chilling sensation of another Reaper.

At first, nothing pinged on my radar. I was just surrounded by cold, empty blackness, with pinpricks of light indicating the dead.

Then, on the horizon, I saw a bright spot wreathed in

light, which had earned more than one of us the nickname of the *Angel of Death.*

There he is.

Keeping my attention trained on the glowing light, I stepped through the shadows and emerged next to Shelton in one smooth motion. The shadows folded back while I fought the urge to punch the air in triumph. I still had it.

Instead, I examined my surroundings. It looked as though we were inside an abandoned house. The walls were damp, the floor equally so. No wonder I hadn't known where he was if he'd been skulking around one of the town's flood-damaged corners.

Noticing me, Shelton spun around so fast that I took a step back in case he swung his scythe at me. "What are you doing here?"

"Looking for you." I did my best to ignore the instincts telling me to dive for cover. "A local ghost has vanished. That's two of them now."

"I thought you weren't an active Reaper." His eyes narrowed. "Unless that was a lie?"

"You showed up in town right before two ghosts vanished from the inn where I live," I said. "No ghost has ever gone missing here before now."

"I had nothing to do with it," he insisted. "And how do you know no other ghost has vanished in town before now? You haven't lived here that long."

"Have you been asking about me?" Defensiveness crept into my tone. "Who told you that?"

"Everyone knows you're new in town," he said. "Though I'm hearing from the local coven members that you're a meddling troublemaker."

"Hey!" I said indignantly. "The former coven leader was a criminal involved in covering up two murders. I won't apologise for getting her kicked out of town."

And I'll do the same to you if necessary.

Whatever he was doing here, it didn't exactly look innocuous. Most people did not go traipsing around old houses in their free time unless they were looking for trouble. Or ghosts.

"It sounds to me like you're a busybody who had no business getting involved in coven affairs to begin with," he said. "And now you're doing the exact same thing again."

"Look, you're lurking in an old house," I pointed out. "Give me one good reason you might be in here that doesn't involve breaking the law."

"I notice you don't have your detective friend with you," he said. "Haven't you told him what you are? Or do you pretend to be human?"

Okay, that was uncalled for. "He knows perfectly well what I am, but I decided to give you the benefit of the doubt before I called the police to come and haul you in for questioning."

"I don't think that's what you did," he said with a nasty smile on his face. "I think you wanted to keep him away from this side of your life because you're afraid he'll run if he sees the truth of what you are."

Anger flared inside me. Who the hell did he think he was?

"Okay, first off, you have no business making judgements about my personal life," I said. "And second of all, maybe I left him behind so I could confront you without the police being involved. I've given you more than enough chances to explain yourself, so…"

I pointedly pulled out my phone. At once, shadows flooded the room, folding outwards from Shelton's feet. "Don't force me to act against you, Maura."

"Don't act as though you weren't trying to provoke me," I warned. "Even if you were being polite, you're the one who's skulking around a flood-damaged house and not offering up an explanation. Two victims of the floods have vanished. Did someone hire you to get rid of their ghosts, or did you act of your own accord?"

"Did someone *hire* me?" He sounded disgusted at the very idea. Maybe I'd got the wrong end of the stick after all. "What kind of nonsense is that?"

"I assumed you were a rogue, since you won't admit who you are or what you're doing here," I said. "If I'm wrong, who are you working for? It's not like there's a Reaper equivalent to MI5 or whatever. The council won't strike you down for telling me."

"Maybe I don't trust you."

"Wow." I arched a brow. "And that's supposed to make me believe you have benign intentions? If you won't tell me who sent you, then why are you in this house? I didn't see any ghosts."

Not that the ghosts had been the priority when I'd hopped through the shadows. I'd been more focused on landing next to the Reaper. But I hadn't seen any other glowing presences nearby. Surreptitiously, I let the shadows fold around me, keeping my eyes open for any spiritual presence. Shelton took a step forwards, the scythe in his hands again.

"Hey, I'm not threatening you," I said. "Just checking out the scenery."

He didn't lower the scythe. The threat was as clear as daylight. Unfortunately, now was not the time for a fight. Using my Reaper skills to step halfway across town had taken some energy out of me, and I was in no shape to fight with someone who had access to the full arsenal of Reaper talents. Most of mine were still dormant.

Instead, I let the shadows drop. "All right. You get on with whatever you're doing. I'll do my own thing. Go on."

He took a step back, and when I moved in the same direction, he scowled. "You can't follow me around."

"I'm not following you," I said. "I'm doing my own thing, like I said. Put the weapon down, and I'll step away."

When he lowered the scythe, I did exactly that, scanning my surroundings. The dilapidated room wasn't exactly a stunning vista, but maybe I could get a clue about what he was doing here from within the land of the living. I walked through the room, not quite daring to turn my back on him. I didn't trust him not to strike me down if I did so, and despite his outrage at my suggestion, maybe he *was* a rogue. No Council Reaper would set foot in a place like this unless they were doing grunt work for another—

Uh-oh. Had someone more senior sent him here? Would a higher-up Reaper show up in town next?

As I was turning around to look at him again, I spotted the residue of some kind of herbal concoction on the floor. I crouched to examine the remains, and suspicion flared up inside me. I knew the smell of that particular concoction… someone had summoned a ghost.

Which ghost? I hadn't considered it before, but it wasn't impossible that someone had used a summoning spell and drawn Eric and Lara's ghosts into this house before banishing them. It'd certainly explain why we'd found no clues at the inn. Not that I could see any traces of a banishment spell, but maybe it was elsewhere in the house.

I trod around the room, then I jumped into the air with an exclamation as the Reaper appeared out of the shadows beside me.

"Did you set up that spell?" I shuffled away from him, my heart racing against my ribcage, and jabbed a finger down at the smudged remains of the spell. "Did you summon a ghost in here?"

He scoffed. "If I wanted to summon a ghost and then banish it, I wouldn't need to waste money on herbal concoctions, would I?"

"I guess not." Which meant someone else had been here. A witch or wizard, no doubt. But who? And which ghost had they summoned?

The Reaper studied me but didn't speak. I tilted my head on one side. "Why're you looking at me like that?"

"No reason."

"There is," I said. "Like there's a reason for you being in town to begin with. If you're not here to play vigilante against the local ghosts, then why? Did you know someone had conducted a summoning or banishment here in this house before you came here?"

"No."

Finally, an answer. Maybe not an honest one, but at least he'd said something that wasn't an insult or an evasion. It was an improvement of sorts.

"Then what were you looking for?"

The question hung between us, but he didn't answer. Instead, he stepped into the shadows and was gone.

I stared at the spot where he'd vanished for a moment. The Reaper might be a nuisance, but despite his attitude, it seemed he wasn't responsible for our missing ghosts after all.

9

I wasn't inclined to take the Reaper's word for it that he wasn't up to anything nefarious, but there was no point in sticking around the old house with nothing else to be found.

Instead, I returned to the inn, using the shadows as a shortcut with my Reaper skills. This time, I misjudged a little and landed outside the inn instead of in my room. I realised my mistake the instant Carey jumped a foot in the air and dropped her schoolbag. "Where in the world did you come from?"

"Reaper trick," I said. "I can hop through the shadows from one place to another. Sorry I startled you."

"Where'd you go, then?" she asked.

I hesitated for a second before deciding I might as well tell her. I had to face the fact that I was lost, and I could use a bit of perspective from someone who wasn't as biased against Shelton as I was. "I *may* have followed the new Reaper to see where he was hiding out."

Her brow wrinkled. "Where was he?"

"Turns out he was skulking around an old house." I walked with her into the restaurant. "He wasn't best pleased with me for ambushing him, but it's his own fault for being so elusive."

"Who's being elusive?" Allie called from behind the bar. "Maura, I didn't see you go out."

Carey and I walked to her usual table, where she put down her schoolbag. Casper bounded onto a chair, purring.

"The Reaper," I answered, resigned to telling Allie as well. It wouldn't do any harm at this stage.

I gave them both a rundown of my confrontation with the Reaper. While I tried to downplay how close we'd come to swinging scythes at one another, neither of them appeared to be fooled. Allie had to go off to serve a customer as I was finishing my story, but Carey's mouth was open by the end of it.

"Wow," Carey said in a hushed voice. "What was he doing in that house if not banishing a ghost?"

"I have no idea," I said. "As he rightly pointed out, he wouldn't need to use a complicated spell to conjure up a ghost. Or to banish one, come to that. He wouldn't carry a scythe otherwise."

"I guess not," she said. "Weird. You were so sure he was the one who got rid of the ghost…"

"Two of them have vanished now," I said. "Turns out the guy who asked me to find the missing ghost is now missing himself."

"No way," she said. "You mean the second guy who used to be at the academy?"

"Yeah, him," I said. "It's bizarre. On top of that, the

Reaper is weirding me out. I can't think what else he might have been doing in that abandoned house if he wasn't after a ghost, but he refused to tell me a thing, including whether he was working for the Reaper Council."

She blinked. "Does it make a difference if he is?"

"Yeah," I said. "The Reaper Council… let's just say they wouldn't be pleased at the situation in Hawkwood Hollow. They'd give old Harold a stern talking-to for letting the number of ghosts here get so far out of hand, arrange for as many as possible to be banished, and then come after me. If they found out about our ghost-hunting missions…"

Her face fell. "They wouldn't ban you from going ghost hunting altogether?"

"I'm not supposed to use my Reaper skills if I'm not an acting Reaper," I said. "Ghost hunting, the way we do it, is kind of a grey area, but the Reaper Council sees things in black and white. That's one of the reasons I left them."

"They can't stop you from doing whatever you like," Carey protested.

"They can try," I said. "If they just gave me a warning to quit looking for ghosts in my spare time, I'd just argue that I wasn't using my Reaper skills or doing any harm. It would be a pain, but it's not like I'm a high priority with them like I would be if I was a rogue."

"A rogue?" she echoed. "What does that mean?"

"Basically, a Reaper who acts outside the jurisdiction of the council," I said. "An independent ghost hunter who *does* make use of their Reaper skills, for good reasons or bad ones. If Shelton is working with the council, it throws up a bunch of complications I don't need, but if he *isn't* with them, it's almost worse, because it means he's a rogue himself. Either way, it's safe to say the council won't be far behind him."

And then? They'd see the number of ghosts in town and draw their own conclusions. Old Harold would face the worst of it, but I'd take some of the backlash, too. Especially if they found out about Mart.

"So either way, the council is coming here?" she said.

"Not if I can help it," I said. "If he *is* a rogue, I'll recruit Harold, and we'll team up on him. If he's with the council… I'm not sure. He hasn't acted against me so far, so I have no idea what they sent him here for."

Aside from our argument, he hadn't reprimanded me for ghost hunting or even for using my powers to sneak up on him. Instead, he'd taunted me over my potential relationship with the detective, an odd decision for someone who worked with the Reaper Council. Admittedly, Reapers weren't known for their social skills, but my money was on him being a rogue. An odd one, admittedly, but a rogue nonetheless.

"Is he really that much more powerful a Reaper than you are?" she asked. "I mean, if he was about to banish a ghost, could you stop him?"

"I'd give it a fair shot." I didn't want to alarm her, but there wasn't much point in underplaying what we were dealing with here. "I mean, he has a scythe and I don't, but otherwise, we have the same skills. I might be able to get the upper hand on him if I got lucky."

"But you'd need Harold with you to force him to leave town," she concluded.

"I wouldn't say that," I said. "If I borrowed Harold's scythe myself, we'd be evenly matched. Not that I expect he'd let me do that without causing a fuss, but I bet his skills are even rustier than mine. He probably hasn't banished a ghost in years."

Odds were he hadn't seen a fellow Reaper for equally as long; otherwise, the council would have discovered he'd been neglecting his duty and sent someone in to take care of things. Though maybe that was what this was. Who even knew at this point?

Carey bit her lip. "It's better if you wait until he leaves of his own accord, then. If you're sure he's not the one banishing the ghosts in town, I mean."

"I don't trust him an inch, but I'm not certain that's what his game is, to be honest," I admitted. "If it's not him, then we have some other wannabe ghost hunter to contend with."

Which was kind of annoying, I was willing to admit. I'd been all for the idea of chasing Shelton out of town and then washing my hands of the matter. But there were too many unknown factors in this whole affair, and the disappearance of the two teenagers' ghosts surely hadn't been accidental even if the Reaper hadn't been responsible.

"I guess," she said. "It's scary, though, isn't it?"

"I'm not frightened of him." I wasn't—not for myself, anyway. "But if he goes after my brother, then we'll have a problem."

He hadn't banished Mart, though, even when he'd been given the chance to. That wasn't the behaviour of someone here to banish ghosts and nothing more. So what was he doing here?

"I meant the council," said Carey. "It's scary that they

could just stop you from hunting ghosts if they find out you're here."

"I've spent years avoiding them," I said. "Since I left home, pretty much. They say it's not allowed, using my Reaper skills, but it's not like they could police my every movement unless they set a tail on me. It's not worth the effort for them to do that when they have actual rogues to chase."

Carey's expression cleared. "In other words, we need to get rid of the new Reaper, and then things can go back to normal?"

It wouldn't be that simple, but I nodded. "Pretty much. Whether he's involved with the two ghosts' disappearances or not, the quicker he leaves town, the better."

She gave a nod. "Then should we ask old Harold to help us send him packing?"

"He's being almost as elusive as Shelton is," I said. "Even the detective hasn't been able to get him to answer the door."

"Speaking of the detective, aren't you going out with him tonight?" Carey said.

"Nah, he has to get back to work," I said. "And make excuses for why he dug out the files on Eric and Lara's murders."

"He did?" she said. "Wow, he must really want you to spend time with him if he went as far as to delve into the files of an old murder case."

"Maybe," I allowed, "but I think the case is relevant to what's going on now. Why would both ghosts vanish at the same time?"

"Weird," she said. "They died at the same time, though,

right? And their murders were never solved. That's got to be the reason."

"Seems that way." Yet few other people knew their deaths might not have been accidental, or so I'd thought. And none of my suspects had been at the inn when Eric had disappeared.

There was, however, one person who could be in any place at once if he wanted to. We might have come to an agreement, but I wasn't striking the Reaper off my suspect list just yet.

———

The endless list of questions I needed to ask circled through my mind all night, and I woke up to the sound of Mart singing loudly with the shower running at full blast. At least he hadn't flooded the bathroom this time around.

I had an early shift, so I got on with work while I mulled over who to speak to next. Oh, and how and when to mention yesterday's little excursion to Drew. When he messaged me and asked if I was free, I texted back saying I wanted to talk to him, crossing my fingers that he wouldn't get too annoyed with me for leaving him behind to go chasing the Reaper. Okay, Drew would never stop me from doing as I wanted, but the fact that I'd gone after a potentially dangerous individual alone was bound to rub him up the wrong way.

Realistically, though, nobody but a fellow Reaper would have been able to take Shelton on if it came to it. I wasn't certain I could get even Drew to understand that. He didn't know just how dangerous a fully operational Reaper could be.

And whose fault is that? You didn't tell him.

I shook the thought away, blaming my moment of insecurity on Shelton for taunting me by bringing up some of my biggest concerns about dating a non-Reaper. The secretiveness, for instance. But I hadn't lied when I'd said the Reaper Council had no hold over me whatsoever, and that was why I'd started dating Drew without fearing repercussions.

The problem was more likely to come from more personal issues stemming from my Reaper identity. Like my propensity for taking risks that would kill a regular person. Or my creepy ability to summon up Death anywhere I wanted to. But I'd done both, and Drew still hadn't run away. Not even when I'd brought up the rule about not dating non-Reapers during our first date. He'd even said he wanted to see me again, even if he hadn't committed to a particular place and time. That ought to be worth something, right?

My phone buzzed with another message from Drew, saying he was on his way over. My heart gave a flip, and I sternly told it to calm down. For all I knew, my abrupt excursion across town to see the Reaper would be the last straw for him.

Ten minutes later, Drew entered the restaurant and walked over to me. "Hey, Maura."

"Hey," I said. "Want coffee?"

"Sure," he said. "Same as usual. You said you had something to tell me?"

"Yeah." I busied myself making our drinks while I debated how to broach the subject. Once I gave him the coffee, I settled behind the bar and took a long sip of my own drink.

"So," I began, "I may have found our Reaper yesterday."

His brows shot up. "You went looking for him again?"

"Not the way we did," I added hastily. "I can use my skills to track any other Reaper if I want to, and I got fed up waiting for him to show his face. So I stepped through the shadows and cornered him where he was hiding."

"Whereabouts was he, then?" he asked.

"Inside an old house." I ran through what I'd discovered there, including the strange piles of herbs and the general sense that someone else had been looking for ghosts there. Someone who wasn't the Reaper. "It's bizarre, I'll say that much."

His brow furrowed. "Someone used a spell to summon a ghost into the house? A witch or wizard?"

"Must have been," I said. "Which is something we didn't think of when we were looking around here for the perpetrator. If they summoned the ghosts of Eric and Lara somewhere else in town using a spell, they wouldn't have had to be anywhere near the inn to get rid of them. They could just summon and banish them within the same place, and nobody would know."

Which expanded our list of suspects to include the entire town. Not ideal.

"Are you sure the spell you found in that house was used on those particular ghosts?" he said. "Would there have been some kind of banishment spell, too?"

"I didn't find one," I admitted. "I suppose they might have done the banishment elsewhere in the house, but I didn't search the whole place. Maybe I should have, but that Reaper annoyed the hell out of me when he ran off."

"And are you sure the Reaper himself was telling the truth?" he asked.

I shrugged. "He was being evasive, I'll say that much. He said that if he was here to banish ghosts, he wouldn't have needed an elaborate setup like that, and… well, he's right. It makes no sense. I can't overlook that. He has a scythe, after all."

"But those two ghosts were still victims of the same murderer," he said. "Do you think that's why they vanished?"

"I'd feel more comfortable saying yes if the Reaper told me why he was in town, if not for that reason," I said. "He wouldn't tell me. Said he didn't trust me."

Given his reaction when I'd accused him of being a rogue himself, it made sense for him to have reacted like that if he thought I was working against the council. Which couldn't be further from the truth, but if he was with the council himself, he couldn't possibly know who I was unless he'd had direct contact with my father or with someone who'd met me during my brief time as a Reaper's apprentice.

He didn't know there'd be a Reaper in town when he came here. He couldn't have. Which meant he was being cautious out of natural wariness about potentially being around a rogue. That made more sense, but it also made the oddly personal remarks he'd made to me about my relationship with the detective seem even stranger. Not to mention suspicious.

"Has he spoken to Harold, do you know?" he asked.

"I forgot to ask," I said. "I was too caught up in trying to catch him off guard. I have no idea what his deal is, but if he has any knowledge of the local Reapers, he must have known Harold is supposedly in charge of the dead here in Hawkwood Hollow."

The odds were high that he had known about Harold but not about me, so I made a mental note to add that to the list of questions to ask him the next time we ran into one another. The problem was, of course, that it'd be a little difficult to wrangle information from him when I didn't trust him any more than he trusted me. And therein lay my problem. Aside from his bad attitude, that is.

The detective seemed to consider my words. "He didn't know you were here, though?"

"No, because I'm not an active Reaper," I said. "Every one of them has their name on a list that tells all the other Reapers what their skill level is and which area they're in charge of."

His brows shot up. "Would this Shelton person show up on that list? Can you check?"

"I don't have access to it, since I'm not an active Reaper," I said.

"But does Harold?"

I tilted my head. "I like the way you think. I actually don't know. He might've lost the list or forgotten to keep it up to date…"

But it was somewhere to start. It'd at least deal with the question of whether the new Reaper in town was legitimate, which would take a weight off my mind.

"It's worth asking," Drew agreed. "If Harold will talk to you, of course."

I groaned. "What did I do to deserve *two* grumpy Reapers giving me grief? I realise that it's kind of a Reaper trait, but come on."

"You aren't grumpy," he said. "Neither is your brother, from what I've heard."

"Oh, Mart drove the other Reapers out of their minds

by making jokes all the time," I said. "He got more flak than I did for rule breaking as an apprentice, though he liked getting me into trouble as well."

"Hey!" Mart said indignantly, appearing like clockwork when I mentioned his name.

"It's true, and you know it," I told him.

"Are you sure you never broke the rules yourself?" said the detective, a smile playing on his mouth.

"All the time," said Mart. "She likes to pretend to be righteous, but she was always sneaking around behind the council's back. Banishing ghosts… summoning them…"

I turned back to the detective. "Maybe a little. There were a few good reasons I left them. Aside from my brother's untimely death."

Mart let out a howl and flopped over dramatically in midair. "Uncalled for, Maura. That hurt deeply."

I rolled my eyes at him. "Anyway, the council doesn't know who I am, not really. I was only an apprentice for a short time, and I'm miles away from where we used to live. Shelton doesn't know me. But Harold… I'll see what he says."

At that moment, Carey ran into the restaurant in her school uniform, her hair flying behind her and her eyes wild.

"Hey," I said. "Something wrong?"

"Cris and her friends are hunting for ghosts again," she said.

"Where?" I asked.

"She mentioned this abandoned house down by the river," Carey replied. "Opposite the spot where those kids vanished."

"Near the inn?" Oh, boy. "Do you know where?"

She nodded breathlessly. Drew and I looked at one another for a moment.

"You want to go after them?" he said.

"I think I should, before someone gets hurt." I turned to Carey. "Can you lead the way?"

10

Carey beckoned her familiar to her side. "We're coming with you."

Casper meowed in agreement.

I shook my head. "Don't go following Cris and the others into a creepy house. It's not—"

"Safe?" she said. "I know Cris and her friends. They want to get footage for her blog, and I don't think they've considered the risks at all."

Drew and I took the lead, while Carey walked behind us. She carried her ghost goggles in one hand as though hoping to catch good footage of any spirits we might run into in the house, but I suspected the footage would be the least of our problems if we didn't stop those kids from risking their necks for a cheap joke. Her mother wouldn't be thrilled with me for taking her with us, either, but with a little luck, we'd get to the house and send the schoolchildren home to their parents before anyone else had to know.

The three of us crossed the bridge and walked alongside the river until we reached a street full of abandoned houses that had half collapsed due to neglect. Carey hesitated, scanning the front of the buildings, while a flicker of familiarity stirred within me.

When Carey picked out one of the houses, I peered through the window. "You've got to be kidding me."

"What is it?" said Drew.

"I think this is the house where I tracked the Reaper down yesterday."

How in the world had those kids found this place? The Reaper didn't know the students from the local academy, surely. He wasn't even from this town.

"Are you sure?" whispered Carey, her eyes wide.

"I didn't go outside and check the location while I was there last time," I said, "but I recognise the room."

The old house looked even more dilapidated from the outside, with crumbling bricks and missing roof tiles. Its shattered windows were boarded up, preventing us from seeing who was inside, but I could hear voices from behind the closed door and recognised Cris's ghost-seeing blond friend, Ann, among them. Definitely the right place. Had it been her idea to come here, or Cris's? Or had someone else pointed them in this direction? Given the absence of any ghosts the last time I'd been here, it was anyone's guess.

Drew pushed the door inward, and we headed down the short hallway and turned right. Cris and her friends had gathered in the living room, and several shredded herbs lay scattered on the ground at their feet.

So it's true? Had they been the ones who'd summoned the ghosts here after all?

"What are you doing here?" Cris demanded. "Go away."

"I'm here to stop you from making a foolish mistake," I said. "You were about to summon a ghost, weren't you?"

"What's it to you?" she said. "We can't all snap our fingers and have spirits appear in front of us like you."

"Look, do you even know which ghost you're summoning?" I said. "If you aren't specific enough when you cast the spell, you might get a spirit who's stronger than you're prepared for and who isn't thrilled at being summoned by a bunch of kids. Trust me, this is a bad idea."

Cris's gaze went to Carey. "You told tales on us, didn't you? You called the police and told your friend to come here."

"I didn't call the police," Carey protested.

"The Reaper witch is dating the detective, though," Ann piped up. "So she brought him along to try to scare us off. Too bad it won't work."

Carey's face flushed. "Look, I was worried about you summoning a ghost without thinking it through. Spirits aren't harmless. They can be really dangerous. I've nearly been killed by one of them before. Maura is the expert, and she knows what she's doing."

"Ghosts aside, this old place is falling to pieces," said Drew. "If there was an accident, one of you might have ended up seriously hurt."

Cris glared at him. "We aren't stupid. We were getting on just fine before you got here."

A creak sounded from somewhere above our heads. I looked up at the off-white ceiling, as did everyone else in the room.

"What was that?" Ann asked, unconvincingly.

"What did you summon?" I asked.

Cris blinked. "Nothing. We didn't finish the spell before *someone* interrupted us."

Uh-huh. I wasn't sure I believed her, and I certainly wouldn't be leaving without checking out the source of the noise. Someone, living or dead, was definitely upstairs.

"I'm going upstairs," I said to Drew. "Can you keep an eye on things down here?"

"Of course." He knew my Reaper skills meant I'd be fine even if the whole house came crashing down on me, in theory, but that didn't mean he was keen on the idea of me facing an unknown spirit alone.

"None of you follow me," I warned the others. "In fact, you should leave the house right now. All of you."

"I'm not going anywhere," Cris protested.

"Yes, you are," Drew said in as stern a voice as I'd ever heard from him. "All of you, get out."

He was in full police chief mode, and even the most stubborn person wouldn't dare disobey. The students traipsed out of the house, while Carey hung back, an uncertain look on her face.

As for me, I trod upstairs, following the creaking sound. Had the students managed to summon up a ghost after all? I knew that to summon a specific spirit, you needed something that belonged to the person, and it was pretty unlikely that they had any of the personal possessions of Eric and Lara. That meant they'd probably conducted a random summoning spell in the hopes of drawing the attention of a spirit... any spirit. While the old house probably did have a history of ghosts attached to it, I hadn't been kidding when I'd said anything might have answered their call, from a simple spirit to a full-fledged poltergeist who wouldn't have been able to resist tormenting a few students for a laugh.

I trod gingerly across the floorboards, careful to watch my step in case my foot went through the floor. Been there, done that. Yet I didn't see anything ahead of me, human or ghost. I turned on my Reaper senses and scanned the upper floor through the blanket of shadows around me, but I drew a blank. No ghosts. No living people either, including the Reaper.

Weird. I'd definitely heard a noise that hadn't sounded like the usual grumblings of an old house creaking away to itself. The only other explanation I could think of was that the other Reaper had been upstairs, and he'd used his shadow-jumping trick to sneak out when I came looking for him. Maybe I should have used my scanning ability from the start, but opening the afterlife on top of those kids would have been a bit much, even if they could benefit from getting some sense knocked into them.

If it *was* the Reaper, he wouldn't come back until the coast was clear, so I retraced my steps and climbed down the stairs to join the detective. As I'd predicted, he'd waited for me instead of going outside. Carey and Casper had stayed with him, too, though I wouldn't have wanted to be alone with those kids either.

"Any luck?" Drew asked.

"Nothing," I said. "False alarm, I think."

"There weren't any ghosts up there?" asked Carey.

"Didn't look that way." I walked over to the pile of herbs and dug my heel in, grinding them into the floorboards. "That'll stop anyone else from doing any summoning spells."

Cris's indignant voice came from the other side of the boarded-up window. "Hey! You can't do that."

"We bought those herbs ourselves," Ann added.

"Tough." Job done, I left the house behind Drew, Carey and Casper bringing up the rear. "You should have saved your money instead."

"Go on," Drew said sternly to the students. "Go home to your parents. Did any of you tell your families you were coming here today?"

Mutters broke out among their group. *Guess not, huh.* Not that it came as a surprise. They struck me as the kind of kids whose parents let them do whatever they liked and were then surprised when their teenage children went off the rails. Still, their annoyance was not my problem. As long as I'd stopped them from summoning an angry poltergeist, I considered this a win.

Our group waited for the students to traipse away before leaving the house behind us.

"Shelton didn't come back," I remarked to Drew as we left. "Whatever he was doing here yesterday. Can't say I know why he'd have told those kids to come ghost hunting here, so I'm guessing someone else did."

The house was close enough to the site of those two students' deaths to make me wonder if it'd shown up in a story from the time that I hadn't heard yet, but the more pertinent issue was how in the world they'd found out how to do a summoning spell. It wasn't the sort of thing they were taught at the local witch academy, though I supposed they might've borrowed a book from the library to look it up out of curiosity. I doubted either of the librarians would have expected them to come here and conduct a summoning ritual.

That means I need to head back to the library again.

Drew nodded slowly. "Tell you what, we should speak to the Reaper and tell him there's a bunch of school-children who went to the house after he was there. See how he responds to that."

"Bet that gets his attention," I agreed. "But do you want to do that before or after we ask old Harold if Shelton's name is on the list of Council-approved Reapers?"

"We'll stop at old Harold's place on the way," Drew said decisively. "Once we make sure those kids don't go back to the house."

"Sounds like a plan."

We walked at a slow pace behind the group of retreating students. Drew took the lead, while I fell back to talk to Carey.

"You okay?" I asked her.

"Yeah," she said. "I wonder why you didn't find anything upstairs."

"I guess they didn't succeed in summoning any ghosts," I said. "Lucky for all of us, really. I could banish any ghost if I found one, but it'd be a bit traumatising for Cris and her friends if it turned out to be a violent poltergeist."

She blanched. "Like Mrs Renner."

"Exactly," I said. "She's pretty much the worst-case scenario, but anyone might've got hurt if they'd kept trying that spell, ghost or no ghost."

"So you want to talk to old Harold?" she asked.

"I think you should go back home first," I said. "Before your mother comes after us. Trust me, you won't miss much by avoiding the Reaper."

"Agreed," Drew said.

I half expected her to argue, but she nodded. "Sure. I'll tell her you're visiting the Reaper and you'll be back soon."

Once we'd ensured the students were out of sight of the house, we walked across the bridge and dropped Carey off back at the inn.

"It's up to you whether you want to tell your mum or not," I said. "She won't be amused at me for taking you with me to turf those kids out of the house."

"I'll just say it was like a regular ghost-hunting mission," she said. "She already lets me go on those anyway. It's no big deal. Not like anything happened."

"Fair point." Allie was laid back as far as parents went, though I had an inkling she was just relieved her daughter had any friends at all, even an antisocial Reaper like me. Oh, and the detective. I wouldn't lie; I'd been glad to have him with me when I was confronting those kids.

The authority he wielded had got the students to leave the house with minimal fuss, where they'd probably have argued to the ends of the earth if I'd confronted them alone. Small mercies.

"See you in a bit," said Carey as I waved her off.

After she'd gone back into the restaurant, Drew and I turned around and crossed the river again, heading for the Reaper's cottage. As usual, the place was overgrown with weeds and wreathed in an air of neglect. I knocked on the door, mentally preparing myself for his annoyed shout in reply. Instead, nobody answered.

I knocked again. After no response came once more, I tapped into the afterlife and found nothing waiting on the other side.

"He's not in?" I said disbelievingly. "Does he ever leave his house?"

"Not often," said Drew. "We can check the cemetery. He might've gone for a walk."

I scanned the gravestones littering the hill past the cottage, but the graveyard was small enough that I'd definitely have spotted the grumpy old Reaper wandering around. I did see a few ghosts, which at least was a sign that the new Reaper hadn't run amok in here with his scythe.

"Where's he gone, then?" I remarked. "I have no idea if he took his scythe with him or not, but I'm not going to break into his house and find out. He probably has defensive mechanisms on his door."

"Yes, that isn't advisable," said Drew. "Besides, he doesn't need his scythe to defend himself if need be."

"Guess not," I said. "Right… we'll go and speak to Shelton. If he's anywhere to be found, that is."

Why had old Harold chosen now to go wandering off? Admittedly, he likely didn't know about the kids going to the old house and had no reason to check up on them, but it looked as though we'd have to go and speak to Shelton again without knowing whether he was an official Reaper. Still, we could always talk to Harold later and see what he had to say about our mysterious friend. After all, I didn't want to waste any more time. If Shelton had been connected to the reason those kids had been poking around the old house, then I'd rather find out before they took another risk and someone ended up getting hurt.

Drew and I left the cemetery and headed down the road out of the town, keeping both eyes open for our wayward Reapers. None appeared, but I hadn't expected it to be that easy to pin Shelton down.

"This is ridiculous." I halted in mid step, my patience fizzling out. "Which Reaper do you want to find first?"

"Why?" asked Drew.

"Because I think we'll have to use a shortcut if we want to get anywhere." I took in a deep breath. "Want me to use my shadows?"

Drew's brows rose. "You can bring another person along for the ride?"

"If you hang on tight," I said. "I haven't done it for a while, but if you want to give it a try, I can give you a tour of the afterlife."

"All right," he said. "I think we should talk to Shelton first, since he's our priority."

"This method has its drawbacks," I warned. "If I use my Reaper skills to pin him down, I can't see his physical location until we step out of the afterworld. We might land on top of him while he's showering, for instance."

"Thanks for putting that mental image in my head," he said. "You can't check whereabouts he is before you appear next to him, then?"

"Nope," I said. "But I'm willing to make the sacrifice. I'll warn you if he isn't wearing clothes."

He grinned. "I'm a shifter, remember? I've seen it all before."

I smiled back. "C'mon, let's get this done."

He took my hand, and I turned on my Reaper powers, letting the afterlife surround me. Then we stepped through the shadows together.

11

Luckily for all of us, Shelton was not naked in the shower when we stepped out on the other side of the shadows. Spared that mentally scarring experience, we landed on the country road between Hawkwood Hollow and its neighbouring town. A cool breeze greeted us, and farther down the road, Shelton wheeled around to face us.

"You again?" His eyes went to Drew. "You brought someone through the shadows with you? That's yet another Reaper rule broken."

"I wouldn't have to break the rules if you weren't so determined to avoid everyone, you know." I walked over to meet him. "What are you doing out here?"

"What did I say about minding your own business?" he said.

"I would like you to tell me what you're doing in Hawkwood Hollow," said Drew. "I'm sure you understand why I need that information."

"Not in the slightest," said Shelton.

"You're new in town and a Reaper," Drew elaborated.

"So's she," said Shelton, eyeing me. "You'll have to try harder than that."

Fine, then. "A group of students found their way to the old house where you were hanging out earlier and were attempting to summon a ghost," I told him. "You don't know anything about that, do you?"

"What?" he said. "No. You think I'm a bad influence on the local teenagers?"

"I think you're hiding your real reasons for being here," I said. "And I'm not convinced it's because of your devotion to protecting the secrets of the Reaper Council."

"What I'm doing here is classified," he said.

"By whom?" said Drew. "I'm the chief of police here in Hawkwood Hollow, and I'm the highest authority by default."

"Not where I'm from, you're not."

I folded my arms across my chest. "So you're saying you *are* with the council, but you won't say so directly because it violates whatever promise you made to maintain secrecy. You'd have saved us a bunch of trouble if you'd just come out and said it, you know. I doubt the council would care."

He scowled. "That's not for you to decide."

So it *was* a secret council mission that had brought him here? If he hadn't been so secretive, I might not have suspected foul play. Yet it must have been an important mission for him to ignore the swarm of ghosts inhabiting the town. That was a glaring red flag for most Reaper Council members. What, then, was his real purpose here?

"Two ghosts have vanished," I added. "Both of them were in the same location and vanished shortly after your arrival in Hawkwood Hollow. Since you refused to say what you were doing in town, it naturally drew my suspicion. Can you blame me for jumping to conclusions?"

"Yes," he said. "No true Reaper would make friends with the local ghosts, though given what I've heard about your background, I can't say I'm surprised."

My hands clenched. "You've been asking people about me?"

"Of course I did," said Shelton. "You can't be trusted to tell the truth, and the local Reaper is not a reliable source, so I did some background research on you. You would have done the same."

That's how he knew about my brother. Yet he hadn't banished Mart, not even when I'd sent him to spy on the Reaper. Why he'd chosen to spare Mart when he clearly didn't care for me in the slightest, I couldn't say I had the faintest idea.

"That was the plan, except I'm not an active Reaper, and I have no idea who you are," I said. "A ghost asked me to find his missing friend. Then the ghost himself vanished not long after. Of course I got suspicious about the person walking around with the ability to banish any spirit with zero effort, especially when he refused to answer my questions and had zero respect for local law enforcement." I indicated Drew with a raised eyebrow. "Or the ghosts, for that matter. Do you even know who the two spirits who vanished were?"

"Am I supposed to care about the local ghosts' sob stories?" said Shelton.

"If they were potentially the victims of the same killer, then it's relevant," I countered. "Eric and Lara were thought to be victims of the floods, but if it turns out their deaths weren't accidental, then it looks suspicious that both vanished at the same time. Just saying."

"Not all of us get personally involved with ghosts," he said. "In fact, I might accuse you of inventing the story in order to drive me out of town and disparage the Reaper Council."

I bit back my frustration. "If you speak to any of the ghosts living in or around the Riverside Inn, they can back me up. Yes, I suspected you of banishing the two ghosts, mostly because of the giant scythe strapped to your back and the fact that you won't tell anyone your mission. The town's been this way for more than two decades, and nobody mentioned any ghosts vanishing beforehand, so if a new person walks into town carrying a giant ghost-killing weapon, it's going to draw my attention, isn't it? Even if I wasn't half Reaper."

"If you weren't a Reaper, you wouldn't have got involved."

He just had to keep needling me. Unfortunately, it was starting to look as if he was innocent after all. Despite his attitude, he clearly didn't know who Eric and Lara were or what had led to their deaths or the banishment of their ghosts. He was here for some other reason and had crossed my path by sheer chance, as unlikely as it seemed.

"If you researched my background," I said, "then everything you think you know about me is years out of date. Anyway, if you had nothing to do with the disappearance of the two spirits, then you won't mind my asking if you've seen anything unusual and ghost related around town, right?"

"Unusual in what way?" he said. "If you expect me to help you with something illegal, then you're mistaken."

Drew cleared his throat. "I think we've had a misunderstanding here. I was led to believe you were a rogue operating outside of Reaper jurisdiction. If you want to avoid further incidents like this, then might I suggest letting the authorities know you have important business in town? Even if you prefer not to disclose the reasons for your mission, telling us you're with the council would prevent any further issues."

Shelton's face flushed, but he clearly didn't have a response prepared. He *should* have told the police why he was here, secret business or not, or at least spoken to Harold if not to local law enforcement. If the old Reaper had given a damn, of course, he'd have confronted him along with me, but the blame still lay with Shelton.

"I'll keep that in mind," he said through gritted teeth.

"And if there's anything we can do to help you, then let us know," Drew added.

"Happy to help." I put on a cheery voice, unable to resist taking a jab at him, and the Reaper glowered at me again. "I'd be glad to back you up if you need me to deal with a wayward spirit."

"I don't take assistance from rogues," he said stiffly. "And I hope that you plan on walking back to town on foot, not breaking the law by using your Reaper talents again."

Ah. We were way out in the middle of nowhere, and getting back on foot would take a while. Still, I refused to regret taking a shortcut to find him. At least we'd eliminated one person from the suspect list, albeit the person I had been so sure was guilty that I had zero substantial evidence for the rest.

"Of course." I shot him a false smile. "Have fun with whatever you're doing out here."

And with that, Drew and I turned and began the long walk back to Hawkwood Hollow.

"What *was* he doing out there?" I muttered. "Does his secret mission involve standing in random fields and meditating? He's lucky he didn't end up trespassing on a farmer's property and getting chased off."

"Looks like he's making a phone call," Drew remarked.

"I guess the signal isn't the greatest back in town," I allowed. "But come on. I can't believe he won't tell me what his top-secret business is."

"Isn't that Reaper code for 'looking for a ghost'?" he asked.

I tilted my head. "He's not the only one who did his research, is he?"

"Guilty," he said. "It's true, though, right?"

"Yes, to a point," I said. "He's either hunting a ghost or a rogue Reaper most likely. But given the state of things here, I can't discount the possibility that he's spying on the town and reporting back to the council on the ghost situation. I mean, even if that wasn't his original job, he has good reason to start now, if he hasn't already."

Drew's expression darkened. "Yes, he does, considering the state of things here. Do you think the odds are high that he'll leave and bring more Reapers along with him?"

"Hard to say," I admitted. "I don't think he has a whole team behind him. He doesn't strike me as the cooperative type."

Not that unusual for a Reaper, but he must have had a supervisor who'd sent him on the mission to begin with.

Someone who might follow behind him if he ran into difficulties.

Which, unfortunately, meant that if necessary, I might have to cooperate with the guy. If it turned out whatever he was looking for here was something I could actually help out with, that is. The odds of him accepting my help, though? *Not great. And* the lingering question remained of who'd banished the two ghosts if not the Reaper. The old house he'd been sneaking around was a source of suspicion, too, because we still didn't know why he'd been there—or why those kids had picked it as a target too.

It was growing dark by now, and several more ghosts appeared on the road as we walked closer to the town. At least Shelton's presence hadn't scared them off, if nothing else.

Drew slowed his pace as we neared the high street. "I think it's safe to say we're back at the drawing board as far as the two missing ghosts are concerned if the Reaper wasn't responsible."

"I'll have a think," I said. "Maybe sleep on it."

"Good idea," said Drew. "Or talk with Carey. She comes up with good ideas."

"She does," I allowed. "I hate that she's dealing with so much crap from those kids. I thought they only got into the ghost-hunting thing to bully her and to make her feel bad about her blog, but I don't know if that's all there is to it."

"They weren't even born when the two students died, were they?" he said. "It's horrible to think that they went out of their way to undermine Carey by trying to summon a ghost, but I doubt they had the foresight to banish Eric and Lara."

"True." I exhaled in a sigh. "Guess I'd better get back to the inn, then."

"I'll walk you back."

He did so, and I did my best to enjoy his company and not think too much about the Reaper and how much he got on my nerves. Or those kids, and the question of who'd truly banished the ghosts. The answers would come to me eventually, so I'd have to call on my almost nonexistent Reaper patience until they did so.

We reached the inn, where I found Carey sitting at her usual table with a pile of notes next to the laptop I'd loaned her while Casper napped under her seat. That was a promising sign: it meant she was working on her blog again.

"Hey," said Carey. "You were gone a long time. Did you find the Reaper?"

"Yeah, we found Shelton," I said. "Turns out he *is* with the Reaper Council, on some kind of mission that's so classified he can't tell us what it's about."

Her brow wrinkled. "To do what? Banish a ghost?"

"Maybe," I said. "But he doesn't seem to know about Lara or Eric. I think he's innocent of banishing them."

"Wait, he *didn't* banish them?" said Carey. "Do you… do you think whoever was casting spells in the old house did it instead?"

"I have no idea," I admitted. "This one has me stumped. Drew, too. I was so certain Shelton was up to something. And he is, but it's legal. Even Drew couldn't get him to admit what his actual mission is, either. It's classified, apparently."

Allie walked over. "What's classified?"

"The Reaper's mission," I said. "He claims the Reaper

Council sent him here for a top-secret reason, except he didn't actually say that, because he's not allowed to. I read between the lines."

"He can't tell you, even though you're a fellow Reaper?" she asked.

"I'm not an active Reaper, so no," I said. "Also, he doesn't like or trust me. Whatever his important mission is, he doesn't want my help. Which is fine, because I'd be more than happy to leave him to it if he'd stop getting under my feet."

But the question remained of who'd banished the two ghosts if not a Reaper.

"He's getting under your feet?" said Allie. "I thought you were the one who followed him."

"Okay, you've got me there," I admitted. "I thought he was guilty of banishing those two ghosts, so I felt justified in tracking him down. He didn't exactly act innocent."

"You went to speak to him with the detective?" she guessed.

"Yeah, I hoped he'd speak to an authority figure if not me," I said. "The Reaper Council does like their secrets. We cleared that part up, but we're back to square one as far as the suspects are concerned. I doubt he'll help me find who banished Eric and Lara, anyway. He doesn't care about the local spirits."

"I've been reading those newspaper articles of yours," said Carey. "On Eric and Lara's deaths, I mean."

"You have?" Surprise filled my voice. "I thought you weren't interested."

Her face flushed. "I was always interested, but I didn't want Cris and her friends getting angry with me for going after the same ghosts they were looking for themselves."

"What made you change your mind, then?"

"They saw me at the house today," she said. "They already think you and I are hunting for the same ghosts as they are, so I might as well go with it."

"If you're sure," I said. "I'm not certain there's a link between the house and the two ghosts, but if it means Cris and her friends are going to stop hanging around the inn, I'm all for it."

I looked around the restaurant and saw Mrs Terrence sitting in her usual spot. While I'd learned my lesson about striking up a conversation with her, I did wonder if she'd overreacted to the ghosts' prank after all. Really, it was the most innocuous of the possible reasons for someone to banish the two ghosts, compared to someone trying to cover up a double murder. Which meant it probably wasn't true. The universe was unfair in that way.

"She's being impossible," Allie said in an undertone. "I've remade her drink four times. We *really* need someone else to work here and pick up some of the slack."

"Drew said he'd put a word in with the pack," I said. "But I wouldn't blame him if he forgot to follow up with them, what with everything else we've been dealing with lately."

"The werewolf pack?" she said. "I suppose it can't hurt at this stage. We're not likely to attract anyone else from the coven, or even the witches and wizards outside of it. They don't want to be viewed as supporting Mina Devlin's banishment."

"Is that the problem?" The hold the former coven leader had had over the town was intact even with her gone, apparently.

"I have no idea," said Allie, in weary tones. "It's anyone's guess at this point."

As she walked off to deal with yet another request from Mrs Terrence, I turned back to Carey and the pile of newspaper clippings. "What did you find? Any mentions of that house?"

"No," she said. "I don't know that it's haunted, but the shack where Eric and Lara died wasn't far away, so perhaps that's why Cris thought they might be there. Also, Mina Devlin owned most of the houses in that area, or other people from the coven did."

"Did they?" I frowned. "I wonder why she'd have wanted to pin the blame for the students' deaths on Ed James. I understand why their parents didn't want everyone knowing their kids skipped school the day they died, but why would the coven back them up on that?"

"The coven owned the papers at the time," Carey said. "Anyway, Ed James was the last person to see them alive, and it sounds like he didn't bother going back to check on them when they got the alert about the town flooding. The reports claim he fled the town without telling anyone they were missing."

"I didn't know that part." I moved in to read the article over her shoulder. "I thought he knew they were bunking off school and told tales on them."

Not according to the article. Weird. If he'd been a prefect who'd caught them breaking the rules, why hadn't he reported them to the academy's staff?

Was Ed James not so innocent after all?

12

The next day was Saturday, and I didn't have a shift for once, so I slept in late until the detective texted me in response to the update I'd sent after Carey and I had read over the newspaper clippings. I knew I ought to return them to Debora Lowe at some point, but I'd been poring over every detail to gain any clues about whether Ed had really been innocent and what in the world he'd been doing in the time between his confrontation with Lara and Eric and the start of the floods if he hadn't gone back to school.

I was finishing a late breakfast down in the restaurant when Drew showed up. "You have something new?"

"Kind of." I held up the folder of newspaper clippings. "Carey and I had another look at these yesterday. Turns out Ed James didn't actually tell anyone where Eric and Lara were hiding out after he returned to school. He didn't even go and check on them when they got the news that the river was flooding."

"Really?" Drew raised a brow. "Maybe he figured

they'd have left as soon as the flooding started."

"Maybe." The accusatory tone of the articles had rubbed me up the wrong way, though it wasn't that much of a surprise given that the coven seemed to have been looking for a scapegoat. "I guess the coven *was* in charge of the newspapers at the time, so they might have fudged the details. I also found out the houses near the river were owned by the coven, including the one those kids were exploring. Thought that was interesting."

"I know," he said. "I went digging for information on that house, too, but there's nothing in our records mentioning it."

"Which means no crimes were committed there, not that there aren't any ghosts in the house," I added.

"Exactly," he said. "Granted, I only have access to the police's information, which isn't compiled by a Reaper."

"Reaper files aren't public," I said. "Usually I get that kind of info from the ghost-hunting corners of the internet. Not so much from official channels. Also, even if there *was* something dodgy going on at that house, Mina Devlin might have hidden the evidence."

"I figured," he said. "Regardless, I'm inclined to think the house isn't connected to Eric and Lara's deaths, accidental or not."

"Then why did those kids decide to summon a ghost there the day after Shelton was sneaking around the place?" I said. "I guess they might've followed him there and figured it was a good ghost-hunting spot, but they didn't mention they knew we had a new Reaper in town. What're the odds that he knows a random bunch of teenage witches? Reapers are barely allowed to socialise with each other, let alone outsiders."

Yet a nagging voice in the back of my mind told me I'd missed something else. There seemed no good reason for both Shelton and Cris to end up exploring the same house unless something in particular had drawn them there.

"I doubt they knew one another," Drew agreed. "I would suggest there's another connecting factor we haven't found yet. As for the missing ghosts… I can't say I know for certain how they fit in."

"We never checked if Ed James has an alibi for the ghosts' disappearances, either," I added. "We can't necessarily assume guilt, though, not if we believe him over Mina Devlin and the newspapers, which I'm inclined to."

"And not if he can't see ghosts anyway," said Drew.

"True," I acknowledged. "I'm lost. Do you have any new ideas?"

"Not at the moment. I hoped *you* would."

"I should probably take these newspaper clippings back to Debora Lowe to start off with," I said. "She gave them to me and not those kids. I guess I should be grateful for that, at least."

"I'll go with you," he said. "We can check in with Ed James on the way and see if he has an alibi for the time of Eric's ghost's disappearance."

I had my doubts that he'd be thrilled to get another visit from us, but when we reached the high street, we ran into none other than Ed James himself leaving the library.

I halted in front of him. "Oh, hey."

"You again?" he said, sounding unenthusiastic.

"That's me," I said. "What were you in the library for?"

"Nothing."

"Uh-huh." Before I could question whether it was wise, I pulled out the clippings from my pocket. "Not these?"

He blanched. "What are you doing with those? Are you stalking me?"

"No, I'm looking for gaps in your story," I said bluntly. "Is it true that you never reported Eric and Lara's location to the academy when you returned to school, and you didn't go back and look for them when the town was flooding?"

"I…" He trailed off. "What does that matter?"

"It matters because they both ended up dead," I said. "You said you were a prefect. Why didn't you tell the staff where they were?"

"Because the teacher already knew they were skiving, which is why she sent me after them to begin with," he said defensively. "They refused to accompany me back to class, and I wasn't about to hang around there all day. Then the news of the flooding came in…"

"You didn't go back and check on them?"

"I thought they ran already," he said. "I had to get out of there. You have no idea what it was like. The street was practically underwater. The whole *town* was. I figured that they would have been among the first to notice the floods, since they were hanging out right next to the river."

"And the fact that their ghosts have both disappeared now that the case has come to light again is coincidental?" I said.

"I didn't even know they were ghosts," he protested. "I didn't hear a word until you told me, honest. What are you doing with those articles?"

"Returning them to the person who loaned them to me." I jerked my head towards the library. "What were you doing, asking Debora who she told about Eric and Lara's deaths?"

"Why do you care?" he said.

"Some kids from the academy were searching for their ghosts, too," I said. "Debora's the one who gave them the details. Did she tell you that, too?"

"She mentioned someone was looking into the deaths of two ex-students at the academy, but I assumed she meant you," he said. "Why does it matter to you, anyway?"

"Because Eric's ghost asked me to help find Lara when she disappeared," I said. "I didn't lie. What were you doing after the last time we spoke to you, anyway?"

"What?" he said. "Why?"

"Because Eric's ghost vanished shortly after our visit," I said. "Now they've *both* vanished. Call me suspicious, but I think there's something odd there. Whereabouts were you?"

"I went to the Crooked Broomstick maybe half an hour after we spoke," he said. "Ask them if you like."

"I'll do that," said Drew. "Thank you."

Ed James turned around and walked away, his hands in his pockets. I watched him leave, still feeling wrong-footed.

"That was enlightening," said Drew.

"I'm glad one of us thinks so."

"I was being sarcastic."

"Of course." I rubbed my forehead. "Ed has an alibi for Eric's ghost's disappearance, though. That'll be easy enough for you to check up on."

"Yes, it will," said Drew. "I think it's safe to say he didn't banish the ghosts if he was on the other side of town."

"Then who did it?" I didn't expect an answer, but I was starting to think the ghosts hadn't been chosen because of their link to a particular case and were random victims instead. My thoughts kept running in circles, unable to pin down an answer.

"I wouldn't know," said Drew. "I'm fairly sure he didn't kill Eric and Lara, though. He doesn't strike me as a murderer, and considering the whole town was flooding at the time, it's not implausible that he would have run off without looking back."

"I guess so," I said. "I'll hand these papers back to Debora."

Drew nodded. "I'll text you after I confirm Ed James's alibi, and then we can plan our next move."

"See you later." I waved him off and entered the library.

Debora Lowe stood in the same place as before. She gave me a smile as I walked over. "Hello, Maura. Is there something you need?"

"Thanks for these," I said, handing her the folder of clippings. "I saw Ed James was just in here. Was he asking you about the case as well? I know he was the main suspect…"

"You spoke to him?" she said. "Poor thing had to deal with the backlash twenty years ago, and he got worried when the case came to the surface again. I tried to reassure him that the police wouldn't arrest him without proof, but he seemed unnerved by the idea of his former classmates running around as ghosts."

"They aren't anymore." I wasn't entirely sure why I was telling her, but I was curious to see how she reacted. "That's the problem. Both spirits disappeared. Eric and Lara, I mean."

Her brows rose into her hairline. "Is that… normal?"

"Not here," I said. "I don't suppose anyone's recently checked out a book on how to summon and banish ghosts? Like a certain group of teenagers, for instance?"

Her mouth pursed. "Guilty. In my defence, I thought they were just curious. I didn't know they'd go ahead and try it out themselves."

Great. "I'm not sure why they picked those two ghosts to target, though. Also, I thought they were more interested in filming ghostly activity for their blog, not banishing them."

Or rather, sabotaging Carey's own ghost-hunting ambitions. Would they go as far as to research how to banish a ghost for the purposes of tormenting Carey? Perhaps they would. Cris had struck me as unscrupulous to say the least, but the sheer number of ghosts in town would make banishing them all a difficult prospect even for a Reaper.

"I'm afraid I can't speak to what teenagers like to do in their free time," she said. "I assume their parents aren't aware of their hobbies."

"You probably aren't wrong," I admitted. "What did you say to Ed James, then?"

"I admitted that I may have had a hand in the renewed interest in the case when I humoured those academy students," she said. "With the ghosts gone, I assume those kids will find something else to do, and it'll be forgotten soon enough."

"Not necessarily," I said. "Have they been in here since the last time you saw them?"

"No, they haven't," she said. "I had to apologise to Ed for the trouble, but I hope he can put the unpleasant incident behind him now."

Hmm. "I hope so, but if those kids have a book on summoning ghosts, I don't see them giving up anytime soon. Can't you ask for it back?"

"I rather hoped they'd come back in person so we could have another chat," she said. "Isn't that girl who lives at the inn their classmate?"

"Carey?" I said. "Yes. She's my friend, and those kids are bullying her. That's why they developed this sudden interest in ghosts."

"Well, that's just not on." Her expression turned aggrieved. "I can call their parents—"

"Best not to," I added hastily. "She doesn't want trouble, but I think their parents need to know they're practising amateur necromancy in their free time. I found them trespassing in an old house, trying to summon another ghost, yesterday."

"I think that's more of a matter for the police to handle," she said.

"Guess so." I stepped back towards the door. "Thanks for the help."

I left the library, stepping over the inexplicable barrier of herbs at the door. *Now what?* I hadn't counted on all my theories turning to dust in the space of an hour, but maybe Drew would have some new ideas when we met up again later.

I'd hardly taken three steps when Mart flew up to me, his eyes wide. "Maura, I need your help."

"With what?" I glanced behind me, but the door had closed on Debora, and I was fairly sure she couldn't hear me talking to a ghost.

"That witch, Faith Murray, is back at the inn," he said. "I think she's casting a spell."

"Faith Murray?" I echoed. "Didn't you tell Carey or Allie?"

"They can't see me," he said. "I tried everything—rattling the cutlery, levitating things, the works. They might have guessed it was me but not that I was trying to give them a warning."

"Dammit." I broke into a run. Mart flew alongside me, his expression unusually sombre. I hadn't thought of the possibility that he'd be unable to warn the others when there was trouble at the inn and I wasn't around. "Guess that answers the question of who put those herbs outside the library."

I sprinted across the bridge and towards the inn, spotting a tall figure wearing a pointed hat standing on the riverbank with a pile of herbs around her feet.

At once, I pulled out my wand and cast a freezing spell. Faith's entire body froze on the spot, giving me the chance to run over and kick her pile of herbs over the bank into the river. When she unfroze, she fastened a glare on me. "What are you doing?"

"Getting rid of your spell," I said. "I'm not going to let you cast illegal magic next to the inn. There are innocent people in there—living and dead."

"Exactly!" Mart chipped in, his words provoking no reaction from her. Faith couldn't see or hear him, then.

"I wasn't casting an illegal spell." She scooted over to the riverbank, but what remained of her spell had already been washed away. "You have no idea what's loose in this town, do you?"

I lowered my wand. "What are you talking about?"

She gave me a hostile stare. "I was *trying* to protect this town, but you insist on poking your nose into everything, don't you?"

I frowned. "Protect it from what? You mean the Reaper…?"

She scoffed loudly. "I give up. Deal with it yourself if you think you know best."

"Wait—" I walked after her as she marched across the bridge at speed, but with a wave of her wand, she vanished in a flash of light.

An instant later, the door to the inn opened behind me, and Allie walked out. "What in the world is going on?"

I spun around and faced Allie. "Faith Murray was casting a spell outside the inn."

"A spirit-banishing spell," said Mart, drifting over to me. "Don't forget that bit."

"Where?" said Allie.

I pointed to the dismantled pile of herbs, or what was left of it. "What the hell is her problem?"

Allie strode over to the riverbank. "Where'd she go?"

"She used a spell to transport herself away." I walked up to her side. "My brother came to warn me about her. He said he tried to tell you, but you couldn't see or hear him."

"He's the one who was levitating things around the restaurant?" she said. "I'd better go back in."

"Sure," I said. "I'll have another look around and see if she dropped any evidence."

A nagging voice in my head told me I ought to follow Faith Murray back to the library, but what if that wasn't where she'd gone? If she'd cast one spell, it might well not be the first time she'd done it, either. She'd left those herbs all around the library, too…

"Call the detective, too," Allie called to me as she walked away.

"He's going to message me later," I said. "He's checking Ed James's alibi for when Eric's ghost vanished, but I guess it wasn't him after all. I'll send him after Faith Murray instead. Drew has the authority to arrest her, while I don't."

I fired off a message to him, telling him to keep an eye out for Faith Murray, while Allie returned to the inn. Then I shuffled farther down the riverbank, keeping both eyes out for trouble.

"Over there!" Mart pointed to my left, where another pile of herbs lay scattered around. "She set up another spell. Maybe in case you dismantled the first one."

"What's her issue?" I strode over and crouched to examine the spell. I'd never been top of the class at memorising the uses for herbs with magical properties when I'd been at school, but I wasn't certain the spell resembled a banishment charm. Whatever the case, I'd rather not leave it outside the inn, so I dismantled the heap of herbs and conjured up a bag to scoop them into.

Mart yelled a warning from behind me. I spun on my heel, clutching the bag. "What is it?"

A growl sounded, and a giant beast leapt down the riverbank at me. I pulled shadows around myself by instinct, and the beast flew past me. It landed with more litheness than I'd expect from a beast of that size and veered around to face me again. Its jaws dropped open, revealing slavering teeth, and released a terrifying roar. The sound echoed in my mind, and my limbs froze at the sight of its fearsome shaggy form.

What in the world is that thing?

The creature made another lunge at me. Once again, I dodged to the side, and the giant monster sailed over my head, towards Mart's floating form. He yelped and flew higher, and the beast's snapping teeth missed him by inches.

My heart gave a sickening lurch. The creature wasn't aiming at me but at Mart instead. *I know what it is.*

But it was impossible. Soul-eating hellbeasts didn't just fall out of the sky. They were summoned. I hadn't known anyone else in town had the skills to summon one of those things, much less *wanted* to. Worse, I didn't have any weapons except my wand. The beast was stronger than any ghost, so my Reaper skills wouldn't be able to bring it down, but I wouldn't let it hurt my brother.

I pulled out my wand as the beast leapt at Mart again and cast a free-framing spell. The beast shook it off as though it was nothing. *Uh-oh.*

"Help!" Mart shouted.

Teeth bared, the beast did another flying leap into the air. Shadows folded around my feet as I stepped up and grabbed its flank from behind. I might not have a scythe, but my link to the afterlife ought to enable me to banish it.

I hadn't got into a full-on magical fight in a long time, though, and my grip broke almost at once. The beast snarled at me, but I stood my ground and conjured shadows to my hands. "Stay away from my brother."

The beast turned pitted eyes toward me, recognising what I was. *Come on, then.*

With a leap, it tackled me, knocking me backwards. I used the shadows to break my fall and then threw a wave of shadow in front of me like a shield. Pain reverberated through me when the beast slammed into my improvised shield, but I refused to let go.

"Go away." I used the shadows to give the beast a firm shove, my strength wavering.

When the beast shoved back, I landed on my rear on the riverbank. Biting back a wince, I scrambled for my wand and instead picked up the bag of herbs I'd dropped.

As the beast leaned over me, I waved the bag of herbs in its face. At once, it recoiled. Then it shrank away, disappearing into the distance in several quick bounds.

I flopped against the bank, the world blurring before my eyes. With difficulty, I forced myself to lift my head to make sure the beast had definitely vanished.

"It's gone." Mart's voice was faint.

"Good." I scrambled up the riverbank, flopping onto my front as the herbs fell from my grip. "Man, I don't miss this part of fighting the dead."

"I'm the one who nearly died," he said. "I nearly got my *soul* eaten. It was very traumatising."

"Mm." I hardly had the strength to lift my head. "I guess we know the reason those two ghosts disappeared, then."

Nobody had banished them after all. Something else entirely was going on. Something I could hardly begin to grasp, with my head spinning and my strength fading by the second.

"And I think we also know why our friendly Reaper is in town," said Mart. "I wonder if he'll be happy that we found what he's spent the last few days searching for."

"I think he'll be thrilled," I mumbled.

That was when I passed out.

I came back to alertness when I heard voices nearby. It took me a few long, confused minutes to figure out who they belonged to. Drew… and Allie. My body felt weighted, cold, not at all helped by the dampness of the riverbank.

"Maura!" Drew said. "Are you okay?"

I managed to shove myself into a sitting position. "Yeah."

"I don't think you are." Concern laced his voice, and he walked over to me with his hand outstretched. "Let me help you up."

The hellbeast's attack had drained me, and I was in no shape to argue, so I let him pull me to my feet. I swayed a little, but I managed to stay upright.

He didn't let go of my hand. "Maura, can you tell me what happened back there?"

"My fault," I slurred. "Bit off more than I could chew."

Or rather, the beast had almost bitten a chunk out of

me. *Well, it was more aimed at the ghosts than at me. I'm not appetising enough for it.* A weak chuckle escaped me, and Drew looked at me with a faint trace of alarm in his expression.

"Was it that witch's spell?" asked Allie. "Did it hurt you?"

"Who?" Drew asked.

"Faith Murray," said Allie. "She was setting up some kind of spell outside the inn. Maura's brother fetched her because I couldn't hear him trying to warn me, but Maura said she was going to deal with it herself."

"Whereabouts is Faith Murray now?" Drew asked in a low, dangerous voice that made the hairs rise on my arms and my limbs quiver for reasons not entirely to do with my exhaustion.

"Gone," I mumbled. "It wasn't… wasn't her."

The words tangled together in my mouth. There was far more to say, but the hellbeast… that was a prime example of classified information the Reaper Council didn't want the public to find out about. No wonder Shelton had been so reluctant to tell me what he was doing here. The question was, had the creature run here of its own accord and decided to stick around due to the number of tasty souls for it to snack on, or had someone sent it directly to the inn for a reason?

"C'mon, we'll get inside." Drew gently tugged on my hand and helped me walk to the lobby, which I appreciated. I had to lean on him more than I'd have preferred, but it was that or collapse into an undignified heap again.

"Thanks," I mumbled. "Drained me. Need more practise."

"What did you mean, it wasn't her?" Drew caught my arm as I swayed, and the bag of herbs caught on my feet, making me stumble. "What's this?"

"Faith's herbs," I said with difficulty. "I dismantled her spell."

"I'll take it." Allie stepped in and picked up the bag. "Drew, get Maura up to her room."

I mumbled a protest, but the detective was already steering me towards the stairs leading to the first-floor corridor. I didn't play the invalid well, but my strength was waning even as my head whirled with thoughts.

The beast couldn't have got here by itself. Someone had summoned it here... someone who must have known there was a Reaper in town. Had *I* been the target, or had it escaped into the area and the Reaper had chased it down?

"Which is your room?" Drew asked, indicating the corridor ahead.

"This one." I fumbled in my pocket for my key and managed to unlock the right door. Luckily, the room was fairly neat, since I didn't have many possessions aside from a broomstick and a suitcase of clothes, so I didn't have to worry about the detective seeing anything I didn't want him to.

I collapsed face-first onto the bed, cursing my spinning head for making it impossible to appreciate that Drew was in my room.

"Typical," I muttered into the pillow.

"Will you be okay?" Drew asked from somewhere near my shoulder.

"Sure," I slurred. "Just need to sleep."

"Just as long as you aren't going to drop dead on me," he said. "You had me worried for a moment there."

I'm worried, too. The only person in town aside from me with the necessary skills to summon a hellbeast was old Harold. I highly doubted *he'd* been the summoner, so we were looking at an unknown entity that wasn't one of the people on our suspect list.

"Is she okay?" Allie said from outside the room.

"I think so," said Drew.

I lifted my head and saw Mart hovering nearby, his expression unusually sober. My thoughts stopped on the old Reaper. Old Harold surely wouldn't be wandering around alone if he knew there was a hellbeast loose in town, but who knew, maybe Shelton hadn't told him. He'd been dismissive enough when he'd mentioned the old Reaper to make me think he'd skipped over that step entirely. After all, Harold wasn't an active Reaper either, so maybe Shelton had assumed it wasn't worth mentioning to him.

"Mart," I mumbled.

"Yes?" said my brother.

"Can you tell our grumpy Reaper friend what we're dealing with here?" I asked. "Old Harold... needs to know."

"Of course I will."

I didn't hear another word from the others before everything went black.

———

I slept like the dead. Not in a literal sense, of course. Mart's singing woke me up to prove that point, and by the time I shook off my tiredness, it came as a relief to find that I could stand without falling over.

The restaurant was fairly quiet that morning, affording me the chance to think over the events of the previous day. Coffee and breakfast revived the rest of my energy levels, and I texted Drew telling him that I'd explain everything when we saw one another again. Part of me regretted not saying more yesterday, but I'd been in no fit state to do so, not when I was still reeling from the encounter with the hellbeast myself.

Yet the question remained of who'd summoned the beast and why. Had someone wanted to get rid of all the ghosts in town in one go? Or had this been their inefficient method of disposing of the evidence of Eric and Lara's double murder after all? Surely not, because nobody could control a beast like that, not even a Reaper. Even Harold might not know it was in the area. Or maybe he did if Mart had warned him last night. Besides, living people weren't the targets. Hellbeasts fed on the dead. There was no reason to worry the living.

Except...

Drew's face came to mind. While the hellbeast was no threat to him or anyone else in town, I'd worried him yesterday, and I owed him an explanation. Carey too. Allie had told me she'd been asking about me last night, though she must have opted to have a lie-in today, since she hadn't shown her face in the restaurant yet.

Besides, if I went after the creature again... I had to tell the others first. So they wouldn't follow me.

I stayed in the restaurant after the breakfast tables had been cleared away, helping Allie with miscellaneous tasks.

She didn't push for an explanation about yesterday's events, at least not at first.

"Maura," she said to me when I'd run out of tasks and was cleaning a glass for the second time. "Those herbs you found yesterday…"

"Faith Murray's spell?" I said. "It *was* a banishment spell she was casting, wasn't it?"

"Actually… no, it wasn't," she said. "The concoction did contain herbs intended to repel spirits and other similar beings, but it looked more like a protective charm than a banishment."

"Faith was casting a protective spell on the place?" Had she been trying to keep the hellbeast away? It fitted with her bizarre comments, but how had she known it was here to begin with? I'd been so sure she'd been working against us, and it wasn't as if we actually knew one another. Why would she go out of her way to protect the inn against dark monsters from the depths of hell? It made zero sense.

"It seems so." Allie glanced over at the door. "Ah… there's Drew."

The detective pushed open the door and walked in to join us. Allie moved back, giving us space, for which I was grateful.

"Are you okay?" he said. "I'm surprised you're walking around after yesterday. You looked completely wiped out."

"I did say I just needed some sleep to be good as new," I said. "Really, I'm fine. Back to normal."

"Good." He smiled. "What did you want to talk to me about?"

I took in a breath. "I found out what Shelton the Reaper's classified mission is."

He tilted his head. "Oh?"

"There's… there's a hellbeast loose in the area."

He blinked. "Am I supposed to know what that is?"

"No," I said. "Just trying to figure out how to explain something that non-Reapers are most definitely not supposed to know about. If Shelton finds out I told you, he'll be furious, and he might even set the council on *both* of us. Not to mention poor old Harold."

His eyes widened. "Then why are you telling me?"

"Because you need to know," I said. "Hellbeasts… they're dangerous to the dead more than the living. They feed on spirits and souls."

His eyes widened as the implication sank in. "This beast… it targeted the ghosts at the inn?"

"Seems like it," I said. "Shelton must have come to town in order to chase it down and kill it. Info on those beasts is classified even among the Reapers, so that's why he got so uptight about me asking about his mission."

"You're sure he's not the one who summoned it?" he said.

"No." My shoulders slumped. "Doesn't make much sense for him to be the summoner, though, because he clearly doesn't want to be here. Anyway, it looks like everything else was just a distraction, including the resurgence of the old case and even those academy kids and their ghost-hunting mission. There's no way a bunch of kids summoned that thing."

The odds of it being summoned without a target, however, were lower than I'd have liked. Perhaps it'd been sent after the town's ghosts… or even Shelton himself.

Someone else, meanwhile, had alerted the Reaper Council. That they'd done so without telling me was kind of a sore point, but it wasn't as if I was an official Reaper in anyone's eyes. Harold, as everyone knew, had no intention of doing his job. That left it up to someone from outside the town to come and clean up the mess the beast had left behind. The ghosts were a secondary concern.

"How'd you find out?" he said. "Did you see it?"

"Yeah, it tried to attack my brother by the river yesterday," I said. "I chased it off using my Reaper skills. Took a lot out of me, which is why I kinda passed out."

"You worried me," he said.

"I know." I looked away for an instant. "I'm fine, though. No lasting damage. If it'd got my brother, it'd be a different story."

"Is there a reason someone would set one of those creatures loose in town?" he asked.

I shrugged. "There's a few possible reasons. Of course, it might not have even been summoned here in town. The Reaper might've been chasing it for miles for all I know, but the town's like a buffet for hellbeasts. If it was in the area, it wouldn't have been able to resist coming here to snack on the ghosts."

Drew listened calmly. He was taking this pretty well, but as the chief of police, he'd probably seen his fair share of weird and gruesome sights.

"We'll have to talk to Shelton again," said Drew. "See if he'll cooperate with us now that we know what his mission is."

We. "If you're sure. This isn't going to be easy. I sent Mart to tell old Harold what's going on, if he doesn't already know, so maybe we'll luck out and he'll be supportive for once. He definitely won't want a hellbeast running around town."

On the other hand, I couldn't go after Shelton without turning my back on the inn, which came with its own risks. The beast was still roaming around, looking for spirits to feast on, after all, and if it'd evaded Shelton for this long, then it clearly knew how to hide itself.

"Good," said Drew. "I think we'll need his help if we're to deal with this threat without anyone getting hurt. You definitely shouldn't go after that creature alone."

I guessed he had good reason to assume I'd do exactly that given the chance, so I didn't contradict him. "Hellbeasts can use the shadows to get around, same as me, so it might be anywhere inside or outside the town. I don't think it's near the inn at the moment, though. We'd know if it was."

"Can you track it yourself?" he said. "You drove it off yesterday, didn't you?"

"I couldn't kill it," I said. "I don't have any proper Reaper tools of my own, so I'll need one of our grumpy Reaper friends to do the honours."

"You mean a scythe," he said. "You can't get one?"

"It's not like I can go into Scythes R Us and pick one up."

A smile appeared on his mouth, vanishing a moment later. "You tried to take it on alone yesterday, didn't you?"

"Believe me, I learned my lesson," I said. "I know you don't like it when I don't tell you stuff, but being a Reaper is about more than just hunting ghosts. It's a whole philosophy about not letting anyone in, not accepting help. We do things alone. Hard to break the habit."

"You don't, though," he said. "Not always. You chose to

stay here and help Carey with her blog when you could have left town and returned to the normal world."

"Guess I'm not good at obeying the rules," I allowed. "Never have been."

"I'd never have guessed," he said lightly. "So… what did you want to do? Help Shelton track the beast?"

"If he lets me," I said. "Also, I have no idea what Faith Murray was playing at, but Allie told me the spell she used was a protective charm against hostile spirits. It wasn't for banishing ghosts. She was trying to protect us."

It would have helped if she'd told us that directly rather than vanishing into thin air, but it was beyond me to figure out why she'd even want to use a protective spell near the inn.

"She did?" he said. "Maura… you do remember texting me and telling me she was using some kind of hostile spell on the inn, don't you?"

"Oh." I'd forgotten. "You went looking for her? After you found me?"

"We did," he said. "She refused to answer our questions or plead in her own defence, so we were forced to take her into custody overnight."

Uh-oh. "You locked her up? Is she still in jail now?"

"She is," he said. "Like I said, she wouldn't answer any questions, and besides, I was too concerned about you to check up on her. We planned to question her again later today."

My heart beat faster at his admission of concern about me, even as guilt assailed me at the idea of an innocent woman being locked in a cell overnight. In fairness, I'd kind of forgotten I'd messaged him about Faith's antics in the aftermath of the beast's attack and my consequent brush with death. And if she'd been as belligerent to the police as she'd been to me, then it was no wonder they'd got annoyed with her.

"I guess we should go to the jail and talk to her, then," I said.

Assuming she wasn't too angry at her imprisonment to listen to me. *This might be awkward.*

14

Drew led the way to the police station, through the automatic doors, and into a spacious reception area. The blond shifter receptionist glanced at the pair of us with a puzzled expression as Drew led me into a corridor at the back.

One side of the corridor was dominated by a wide cell cut off by a barred wall. One lone person sat on a bench inside. Faith Murray looked up and shot me a blistering glare, which I had to admit I didn't blame her for.

"Finally saw sense, did you?" she said.

"You know, if you'd actually told me what you were doing at the inn rather than skulking around in the shadows and dropping herbs everywhere, I wouldn't have jumped to conclusions," I said. "What possessed you to take the law into your own hands?"

"That's rich coming from you," she said.

Hey! "What's your problem with me?"

"Aside from the fact that I'm now stuck in a cell?"

Drew cleared his throat. "I hear you tried to pick a

fight with two of my staff when they confiscated your wand. That's not the behaviour of an innocent person."

She leaned back against the wall. "You have a reputation, Maura, and I knew that if I said a word to you about that *thing* that's loose in town, you'd do something reckless the way you did when you drove out our coven leader."

"You're one of Mina Devlin's people, are you?" That would explain a lot.

"I most certainly am not," she said. "But now Hawkwood Hollow is without a coven leader, and as a result, the town's defences are weakened."

"If you're trying to insult Drew and the police's efforts to keep the town safe, then I really wouldn't advise it," I said.

"I think we both know that there are threats that can't be sniffed out, even by a werewolf pack," she said. "Invisible enemies lurk in our midst, and we are now without a strong coven to defend us. Instead, the police waste their time locking up the likes of me."

"I have two people claiming you punched them when they tried to bring you in," Drew pointed out. "You'll face charges for that, but if you want to avoid further punishment, I'll need you to confirm that you were trying to protect the inn using those spells and not cause harm."

"You already know the answer to that," she said. "I was *trying* to keep that abominable creature from causing any more damage than it already has."

"Why would you cast a protective spell next to the inn?" I asked curiously. "I mean, if you aren't my biggest fan, why would you want to keep me safe?"

"Who said I only tried to protect the inn?" she said. "If

you were thorough in searching the town's boundaries, you'd have found a number of similar spells. That's why the creature has caused less damage to the local spirits than it might have."

But it targeted those two ghosts.

"Did you call the Reaper to town?" I asked her. "I know what Shelton is chasing now, and I might even try to help him find it if he lets me. But I need to know who summoned it and who is on my side."

"You're wasting your time with me," she said. "Both of you. It'll be back."

Then we'll have to find it first.

Drew exhaled a sigh. "Maura, do you want to finish this later?"

I sensed that prolonging the conversation would be unproductive too. "Sure. We'll find the Reaper."

Faith made a noise of protest, but Drew cut through her. "I will send someone to talk to you, but if you try to fight my detectives again, you'll find yourself in trouble. Is that clear?"

Turning our backs on her angry mutters, we returned to the reception area.

"Is there a way for you to confirm if she set up similar wards around the rest of town?" I asked Drew.

"I can certainly send someone to have a look around the borders and check for the same kinds of spells," he said. "However, I can't say I like her attitude."

"Nor me," I said. "I wasn't a fan of what she was saying about the coven, either. Also, if she knew the beast was loose in town, why not just tell me? Or Shelton, assuming she didn't call him herself, that is."

"That's exactly what I was wondering myself," he said.

"I'm not sure I trust her word, but I think finding the Reaper should be our priority."

"Yeah, same here," I said. "Before the beast comes back. Not sure if Shelton's in town or if he's wandering around a field again, though."

"Me neither." He walked with me through the automatic doors and out into the street. "We can walk, or we can use your shortcut method, if you don't mind."

"I like the way you think," I said. "Want to take a trip through the shadows again?"

"I'd like nothing more." He stepped to my side, and my heart skittered at his close proximity as he took my hand. There was more tension there than before now that we both knew there was a small chance we might run into the hellbeast on the other side, but his expression held nothing but faith in me.

I let the shadows of the afterlife surround me and gave the area a quick scan. Seeing no signs of anything hostile nearby, I fixed an image of Shelton's face in my head, and we stepped through the shadows with no resistance, landing beside the Reaper in an empty street somewhere in the north of town.

"You again," said Shelton. "What is it this time?"

"I know what your mission is," I said to him. "Because it decided to attack my brother and me."

"You *what?*" he said.

"That hellbeast you're chasing," I said. "It attacked my brother at the inn last night. I had to send it packing."

"You banished it?" he said.

"No, it ran away."

He swore. "Of course it did. You had to make life more difficult for me, didn't you?"

"It's not always about you, you know," I told him. "It jumped me after I caught Faith Murray setting up a protective charm outside the inn. Since she refused to actually tell me what she was doing, I assumed she was launching an attack on the local ghosts. Turns out she was protecting them instead, but she won't admit why."

"I'm not surprised given the level of chaos you've already managed to cause," he said.

Unbelievable. "I'm not the one who set a hellbeast loose in town. Do you know who did?"

"No." The corners of his mouth turned down. "If I did, I'd have caught them in the act and called in the council to shake some sense into them."

"Why has it been so hard for you to track it down?" I queried. "This is a small town. There aren't exactly a ton of hiding places."

"I'm aware of that," he said. "If you know anything about hellbeasts, you'd know they're experts at hiding inside the shadows of the afterworld to avoid detection. I tried checking the major spirit hotspots, and when that failed, I went back to the site of the summoning."

I stared at him. "What, that's why you were at the house?"

The remnants of the summoning spell we'd found had been used to summon the monster that had attacked Mart, not a ghost at all. The image of Carey's classmates from the academy came to mind, and a chill raced down my back. They'd definitely been meddling with something bigger than they knew, but surely even they weren't foolish enough to summon a deadly monster from the depths of the afterlife. Right?

Shelton grunted. "As you may have gathered, I've got a job to do that doesn't involve appeasing your curiosity."

"It's not my curiosity that I'm worried about," I said. "The monster you're chasing has already devoured two ghosts near the inn, and I refuse to let my brother be next. So yes, I'm willing to do anything to get rid of that creature. Even work with you, if you can believe it."

"I can believe it, but I won't accept it," he said. "You're a rogue."

"I'm not—" *Oh, forget it.* "Maybe a rogue's exactly whose help you need, considering you're having so much trouble tracking that thing on your own. Don't you have bait or something?"

"Bait?" He tilted his head. "This entire town is bait."

My hands clenched. "Are you implying you used the town's ghosts as bait to lure in the beast?"

"Did I say that?"

Argh. We might have been on the same side, but I still had to suppress the urge to give him a firm thwack on the head.

Drew cleared his throat. "If I might make a suggestion, I'd like to assist with this mission of yours. I assume that since we figured it out on our own, you haven't broken the Reaper rules by telling us."

"Shifters can't see ghosts," he said flatly.

"But I have the authority to tell you to leave town." The hint of a growl entered Drew's voice. "Regardless of your mission."

"If I leave, you won't get rid of that thing on your own," said Shelton.

"Try me," I said. "I did a decent enough job of sending it packing yesterday. If old Harold let me borrow his scythe, I could deal with it in a more permanent manner."

"Unless you're willing to use that brother of yours as bait, you'll never corner that creature," he said.

"I didn't need bait for it to show up at the inn before," I retaliated. "Also, with Faith Murray locked up in jail, there's no longer any defences on the place either."

"You what?" he said. "You want to use your home as bait instead?"

"No, but the beast seems fixated on the place already," I said. "If we corner it outside the inn, I bet that between us, we could take it down. If you're willing to let me help you, that is."

He was silent for a long moment. "I suppose it's easier than trekking through the afterworld, hoping it'll show up, given your propensity for using your Reaper skills without the permission of the council."

"I don't use them *that* often," I said. "Only in emergencies. I don't know about you, but I'd say this situation definitely qualifies as an emergency."

"Yes, it does, but the more you use those skills of yours, the more trouble you draw." He shook his head. "We're wasting time. If you want to risk your life, it's on you."

"You should know all Reapers are more resilient than most, even me," I said. "Does that mean you want to come with us to the inn to wait for the beast?"

A moment passed. "I'll give you an hour. If the beast doesn't show up, I'll handle it alone."

"All right, then." Drew and I would have to turn our powers of persuasion on him again if time ran out before the beast showed up, but that could come later.

Now all we needed to do was go back to the inn and wait… but there was Mart to consider as well. Maybe I'd send him to hide out with old Harold. Not that I expected the retired Reaper to put *his* neck on the line, even if he had a scythe where I didn't and was consequently better equipped to fight off a hellbeast than I was. I'd be reduced to using my bare hands if I didn't convince Shelton to come and help me.

All the more reason to stay on his good side, then.

Shelton didn't speak a word to either Drew or me as we walked back to the inn. I hadn't asked Shelton if Faith Murray had been the one who'd called him to town, though she hadn't offered an explanation herself. Including how she'd known the hellbeast was in town to begin with, come to that. *She* wasn't part Reaper.

The one thing we did know was that the beast had been summoned in that old house, which had also been where those kids had gone hunting for ghosts. We'd have to deal with that part later, because we had one chance to get the beast into our trap. While I preferred not to risk the inn's safety, I knew I'd feel a lot easier tracking the summoner if we dealt with our runaway soul-eating monster beforehand.

At the Riverside Inn, I found Allie pacing outside the front doors of the restaurant.

"Have you seen Carey?" she asked me. "I think she went out, but I didn't see her."

"She went out alone?" Right, it was Sunday, so she didn't have school. "I haven't seen her around."

Not that I'd been looking. A shiver of unease went down my spine.

"She's not answering my messages, either," she added.

"I'll ask Mart." I walked into the lobby, scanning the area for my brother. "Mart?"

My brother appeared out of thin air. "Back already?"

"Have you seen Carey?" I asked. "Allie said she went out alone."

"I saw her heading downstairs, yeah," he said. "I assumed she was meeting you."

"I didn't know." My heartbeat quickened. "I think… damn. Those kids from the academy aren't plotting another ghost-hunting mission, are they?"

"How should I know?" he said. "Want me to go looking?"

"No!" I said. "I mean… can you please go back to your room and stay in there? I think that beast will come back to the inn, and we intend to catch it before it does."

"You'd better." He spoke to my retreating back as I ran outside to join Allie again.

"Mart said he saw her going out alone. She's not going after those kids again, is she?"

"I hope not." Her expression shadowed. "Were they planning another trip to that old house?"

"You'd think they'd have learned their lesson after last time."

Okay, nothing had actually happened the last time, though given that I now knew about the hellbeast in town, they'd had a lucky escape. More to the point, if Carey had followed them, or even if they'd forced her to go with them… no, I couldn't risk Carey's safety. And I wouldn't ask Allie to take the risk either. Or Drew.

I returned outside and walked over to Shelton. "Change of plans. I have to go somewhere else first, but you and Drew can stay here and wait for the beast."

"What do you mean by that?" he said. "I thought you wanted to lure the creature into your trap."

"My friend Carey might be in trouble," I explained. "She's been dealing with these kids at the academy… they're the ones who broke into the old house where I found you. They're obsessed with hunting for ghosts, and I think she might have followed them again."

"They were at the site of the beast's summoning?" He swore under his breath. "Remind me never to listen to your suggestions again."

"That's enough," Drew said sternly. "Maura, do you think there's a good chance they ran into the beast?"

"If they're back at that old house?" I said. "That's where it was summoned. I don't know if it's likely to return, but I'd say there's a fair chance they're up to no good. I can set up some wards on this place to make sure the beast doesn't come here while I'm gone, but you two—"

"I'm coming with you," Drew interjected. "If there's any chance of you running into danger, then I won't stay behind."

I should have known he'd be obstinate. "Drew—"

"You can't do a thing against that beast," said Shelton. "Either of you. You'd need a scythe to even touch it."

"I'll take my chances," I said. "I have to help Carey."

15

Ignoring Shelton's annoyed huff, I took off at a run, heading across the bridge and towards the house I now knew had been the summoning site for the beasts. I should have guessed those kids would return at the first opportunity, but if they'd put Carey in danger, they'd get more than a stern talking-to next time around. Maybe I could ask Drew to lock them in a cell, like Faith Murray, to shake some sense into them. That could come later, though, once I knew Carey was safe from harm.

I skidded to a halt in front of the old house, hearing voices behind the door. *I should have known.*

"Can you wait outside?" I asked Drew. "I'll see if they summoned anything before turfing them out."

He didn't look thrilled, but he said, "Fine, but if I hear anything that concerns me, I'm coming in."

Kicking the door inward, I entered and made straight for the living room. Cris and her friends gathered in a huddle… and Carey was with them, too, looking pale and terrified.

"Hey!" I said. "What the hell are you doing?"

Cris glanced at me. "Go away. We don't want you here."

"Tough," I said. "Why'd you bring Carey with you, then?"

"She's the one who followed us," said Cris. "She's always getting in our way, so we decided to let her come and see it for herself."

"See what?" I said. "What are you doing here? If you want a ghost, there's a few dozen other possible places in town for you to go looking where you won't run the risk of the house collapsing on top of you. Why did you pick this one?"

"We're not looking for ghosts, moron," Cris said.

I raised a brow. "Then what're you looking for, mildew?"

"Do you like pretending to be stupid?" she responded. "I don't know how you stand those ghosts being around all the time, but I've had enough of it."

"What did you expect from a haunted house, then?" I tried to catch Carey's eye, but she'd dropped her gaze. "Also, you can't even *see* ghosts, can you?"

"This house isn't haunted," Cris proclaimed. "That's why we picked it. Anyway, soon, nowhere else in town will be either."

Incredulity bled through me. "Are you implying you want to banish every ghost in town to get back at Carey, who never did anything to harm you in her life?"

"What's it to you?" said Cris. "You're the one who spends her free time hanging out with the biggest loser in our class. We're going to get rid of the ghosts, and that'll be that."

"And did you make that decision yourself?" I said. "Was it your idea? Or did someone else put you up to this?"

They couldn't have concocted this scheme themselves, surely. No matter how confident they might be, they didn't truly know what they were messing with.

I took a step forward when Cris didn't answer, and my feet caught on a pile of herbs. *A summoning spell.* They'd set up a new one—which meant they'd had the intention of summoning even more hellbeasts in order to finish the job and wipe out the town's ghosts.

A growl sounded, raising the hairs on my arms. I arched a brow at Cris and Ann. "Please tell me you didn't use that summoning spell."

"So what if I did?" said Cris. "Bet you've done the same before."

"It's not a ghost you summoned," I said. "And no, I haven't summoned up a soul-eating beast from the depths of hell. I'd like to think I had a bit more sense than that even when I was your age."

The growling noise deepened, and a large, shaggy form slipped into the room, followed by another. Oh, boy. *Three* hellbeasts circled the room, their jaws slavering. My body tensed, shadows rising into my hands. I hadn't even been able to take on one of those things alone, let alone three. *Why didn't I borrow old Harold's scythe on the way here? Or ask for his help? Yet even a Reaper in their prime would have difficulty handling three beasts at once.*

Cris's smirk wavered. "I didn't know it was still in here."

"You can't have thought you had that thing under your control, can you?" I said. "Even Reapers can't control hellbeasts."

"You can't?" said Ann.

"She's lying," said Cris.

"She's really not." Carey tried to edge towards me, but the beasts continued to prowl around their group, and just because the kids were alive didn't mean the creatures couldn't cause them any harm.

"Call them off!" Ann yelped.

"Who, me?" I said. "I'm not the one who summoned them."

"I thought Reapers could control the dead!" Cris tried to run, but one of the beasts got in the way. Its jaws opened wide, and I didn't stop to think. I stepped through the shadows and emerged in front of the beast. Its heavy body slammed into me, and I staggered back under the creature's weight. Shadows formed a shield between me and the beast, but the other two walked free, prowling around the others. If there'd been any ghosts in here, they'd be screwed, but in the absence of any other targets, those kids might be in real trouble.

Then the door flew open behind me, and Drew sprinted into the room. *No. Drew, stay back!*

The beasts all turned his way, distracted by the noise, and I shouted a warning as one of them ran at him—only to miss its target entirely.

Drew had vanished, and a wolf had appeared in his place. He roared, leaping at the creature, and the pair of them rolled around on the floor, pawing at each other. I watched in mute horror, not daring to intervene in case I made things worse. His motion had knocked the other two beasts off balance, but they soon recovered, growling at the detective. Dammit, I couldn't watch him get hurt, either.

I grabbed my wand and cast a quick spell. A cloud of darkness fell over the two remaining beasts, and while they couldn't be harmed by magic, I'd rendered them temporarily blind. One skidded to a halt, pawing around in search of a target. The other stopped pacing, growling under its breath, while Drew got the upper hand on the third, pinning it down. With all three beasts occupied, I turned to the cowering students.

"Get out!" I told them. "Go on, run, all of you. If you see one of the Reapers, send them my way. Otherwise, I'd advise you to run before it's too late."

Without the help of a genuine Reaper, all I could do was stall the beasts until backup arrived. Not much of a plan, but I refused to let anyone else get hurt.

Carey grabbed Cris's arm and tugged her towards the door, while Ann and the others unfroze, fleeing the room. Two of the beasts began to prowl after them, so I recast the darkness spell before running in front of the exit myself. Drew still held the third beast down, and my heart twisted inside my chest. We could only stall them for so long.

The darkness spell vanished. I raised my wand to cast it again, and all three beasts raised their heads as though listening for something I couldn't hear. Then, without warning, the three beasts vanished as though drawn into the shadows themselves. Drew rolled to a halt, the creature he'd pinned down suddenly absent. Silence fell over the house, while I spun on my heel to look for the missing hellbeasts. They'd utterly vanished from the room.

"What in the world was that?" Had someone called them away? I ran for the door and saw the academy students huddled together in a pack as they made their way down the road, but the beasts were nowhere to be seen.

Behind me, Drew shifted into human form again… completely naked. Heat rose up my neck, and my mind would have plunged into the gutter if not for the direness of the situation.

"Where'd they go?" he asked.

"I have no idea," I admitted, my gaze darting around as he made zero effort to cover himself. "Maybe whoever put those kids up to this. I don't think they decided to summon that beast for the hell of it."

I wished he'd put some clothes on. It was sort of difficult to focus on planning our next move with him standing nude in the doorway without any self-consciousness whatsoever. *Werewolves. Honestly.*

"Do you have a theory on who it might be?" he asked.

"I do." I kept my eyes on his face, with difficulty. "We need to go to the library, but you might want to find some clothes first."

He shot me a grin. "I'll shift again. I haven't got to let my wolf side go wild like that for a while."

And without further ado, he shifted into wolf form and bounded out of the house and down the road, past the startled-looking students.

"Hold on," I called after him. "Unless I get my hands on a scythe, we can't deal with those creatures alone."

Not without one or both Reapers, at any rate. Drew, however, didn't slow, forcing me to quicken my pace to keep him within my sight.

"Where are you going?" Carey yelled after me.

"To find the perpetrator," I said. "Can you go back to

the inn? If you see those creatures again, run and hide somewhere safe. Don't try to fight them."

I picked up speed and caught up with Drew outside the library. The room within was dark, and my shoulders tensed when Drew pawed his way through the door, growling under his breath. I walked in behind him, but I didn't see any sign of the beasts anywhere.

"Wait," I hissed at him. "Stay by the door. I'll have a look around."

Debora Lowe popped up from behind the counter. "You again?"

"It was you, wasn't it?" I said. "Why, though? Seriously, I'm lost. Why'd you summon those monsters, and why on earth did you set those kids up to take the fall? What were you trying to hide?"

Her expression flattened as she realised that I'd found her out. "Something had to be done."

"About what?" I said. "The ghosts? You can't see them."

"You can," she said. "Besides, it doesn't matter to me whether the ghosts stay or leave. I just want *you* gone."

So that was it. She didn't want a Reaper in town. But for what reason? "Did you send the beast after the ghosts at the inn on purpose?"

"No," she said. "Not at first, though it was a handy distraction to keep you busy. I hoped your taste for meddling would bring you face to face with the beast sooner, but I underestimated your tenacity."

My heart thudded against my ribcage. Where had the beasts disappeared to if not here? "What were you trying to hide? Must be pretty dire if you went as far as to summon something from the depths of hell to be rid of me."

She took out her wand in answer. So that was how it was going to be, huh.

"Did you ever do the same to old Harold?" I withdrew my own wand, and Drew growled at my side. "I guess not, since he never wanted to remember the floods."

"If I'd known what you were capable of, I'd have dealt with you a long time ago." She waved her wand, but I summoned up a wall of shadow to absorb her spell.

"You're assuming you're a match for me." I let the shadows drop, raising my own wand. "You didn't call the other Reaper. Someone else did. Faith Murray, right? Did she know what you were up to?"

"Took her long enough to figure it out," she said. "She was easy to handle."

Had she been the one to see to Faith's arrest? She'd told those kids to cast doubt on her actions, for sure… and she was devious enough that I suspected I knew exactly who'd influenced her.

"Did Mina Devlin—" I cut off midsentence as a bookshelf lifted into the air and flew at me, forcing me to jump into the shadows to dodge it. The shelf crashed to the ground, and Debora raised her wand, but Drew pounced on her in his wolf form and tackled the wand out of her hand before she finished casting her spell. She fell behind the desk, and he pressed a paw to her mouth to muffle her yell.

"Where are those beasts?" I demanded. "Where did you send them?"

"Let me go!" she squeaked.

Drew made a growling noise that meant *no.*

"All right," I said. "I'll go and fetch Shelton, and we'll track them down."

Drew growled again as though to warn me not to go back to the inn alone.

"You restrain her," I said to him. "Make sure she's behind bars so she can't summon anything else. Then come and find me. Okay?"

He didn't look pleased in the slightest, but someone had to restrain her, and I couldn't do that and hunt the beasts down at the same time.

Taking a step back from the desk, I pictured Shelton's face and leapt through the shadows. I landed beside him on the bridge over the river—and found myself face to face with a hellbeast. I scuttled backwards, avoiding its teeth by a hair's breadth.

"You!" Shelton bellowed, swinging the scythe and cursing when the beast dodged him. "You didn't mention there were three of them. Were you the one who sent them after me?"

"Of course not," I shot back, conjuring my own shadows to my hands. "It's not like they'd have listened to me, besides. I'm not the summoner."

Too bad they were a force to be reckoned with even with their summoner restrained. The shadows deepened, revealing the door that led into the true afterlife. To get rid of the beasts for good, I'd have to shove them through it—which would be far easier if I had a weapon. Shelton swung the scythe at one of the beasts while I fought hand to hand with the other, having to move fast to avoid its sharp teeth.

The scythe struck one of the beasts, sending it flying backwards. I ran after it, giving the beast a firm shove that sent it the rest of the way through the gaping door to the afterlife. *One down, two to go.* Maybe we *could* do this.

The second beast chose that moment to pounce on the Reaper, sending him toppling off the bridge and towards the tumultuous waters of the river.

I swore explosively, throwing myself to the side to avoid the beast's swiping claws. Shadows filled the space below the bridge, suggesting the Reaper had been able to break his own fall, but his weapon lay out of reach.

I gave a wild lunge for the scythe, my hands closing around the end, and swung it upward. The second creature fell on me then howled in pain when the scythe made contact. I was acutely aware of how close I was to falling off the bridge myself as I fended it off with wild strikes. Damn, I was out of shape. I had no choice but to keep on fighting it off, though, and I couldn't deny part of me had missed the sensation of wielding a proper weapon against the dark denizens of the afterlife. I hadn't missed the tedious parts of being a Reaper, but this? This felt good.

Another swipe of the scythe struck the beast, and I let the shadows spread from my feet, revealing the after-world. The door loomed behind the beast, and with one final swipe, I sent the hellbeast crashing through into the afterlife.

Then a scream rang across the air, and I let the shadows drop so I could see the real world. My heart swooped downward when I saw Carey and the others at the other end of the bridge... and the third beast was barrelling in that direction.

In an instant, I stepped through the shadows and appeared at Carey's side, holding the scythe defensively in front of the others.

Her jaw dropped. "Where'd you get that?"

"Borrowed it."

Behind the beast, the other Reaper managed to pull himself onto the bridge again, but he was too far off to reach the monster or the scythe in my hands.

A firm swipe sent the beast on the defensive, but it was bigger than the other two, and I was tiring fast. My head pounded, the scythe felt leaden in my grip, and Carey screamed my name when the beast tackled me from the side and knocked me to the ground.

Pain spread through my chest as its heavy weight pressed on me. I saw Shelton running in my direction, but the beast was already lunging at the others—

Then Carey grabbed the scythe from my hand and stabbed upwards. The beast recoiled from the weapon, and I wriggled out from underneath it and was back on my feet a moment later. Carey swung the scythe again, and while she missed, the beast staggered back, not seeing Shelton approaching it from behind. Nor the door's outline shimmering nearby.

Seeing I was back on my feet, Carey handed the scythe to me, and I gave the beast another strike. As it staggered back, Shelton gave the beast a firm shove through the door, where it vanished into nothingness.

Breathless, I lowered the scythe. Its owner stomped over to me and all but snatched the weapon from my hands while I slumped into a sitting position. The creatures were gone, and I'd never felt more relieved in my life. Or exhausted. The two of us looked at one another, then Shelton eyed the students. "Go home. Beat it."

"Wait." I struggled upright. "Drew is with the person who asked the students to summon those beasts, but I expect the police will want to speak to them as well."

Cris made an indistinct noise of protest. The others looked too terrified to speak at all.

Shelton looked at them. "*You* summoned those beasts?"

"Debora Lowe told them to," I added. "She's at the library with Detective Drew, though she might be in custody by now."

A scowl appeared on his face. "Right. You lot, come with me. We're going to see the police."

Amazingly, they did, traipsing after him without objecting. Except for Carey, who knelt beside me with an expression of concern on her face. "Are you okay?"

"Just tired," I mumbled. "I'll be fine after a nap."

"Carey!" Allie's voice rang out.

Carey twisted around to see her mother, who ran across the bridge to us and embraced her daughter. While Carey explained what the students had done, I sat down and tried not to pass out. As some of my energy returned, I chipped in to add details to Carey's story.

"There's one thing we didn't find out," I said. "Who called the Reaper to town? Was it really Faith Murray?"

"I know who did it." Mart appeared hovering behind me. "Hey, Maura."

"You left the inn?" I reprimanded him. "You're lucky those creatures are all gone."

"Well, yeah," he said. "I had to when I saw this guy wandering around. Seems he's more resourceful than we thought."

I looked past him and saw Harold the Reaper, of all people, approaching our group on the bridge. "Wait, *you* called Shelton to town?" I said to him. "It was you who tipped him off about the beasts?"

"Yes. Why?" he said, in his usual unfriendly tone.

"He led me to believe that you weren't involved," I said. "Pretty sure he said you were useless and unreliable, actually."

"That sounds like him," he said.

I frowned. "Doesn't that offend you?"

He shrugged. "Nothing I haven't heard before."

"Right." I'd never understand him in a million years. "You might have let *me* know a monster was snacking on the local ghosts."

"I hoped you'd stay out of this one."

"I was the target." I gave him an accusing look. "Didn't know that, did you? Seems Debora Lowe didn't want a Reaper in town."

"Now she has three of them." Mart snickered. "Too bad. She's the one who summoned those things?"

"She asked those kids to do the actual summoning," I said, addressing the old Reaper. "So we have several traumatised teenagers as well as the Reaper Council having twice the reasons to come nosing around here."

"They won't come," said old Harold.

"How'd you figure that one out?" I said. "You *contacted* them."

"I contacted Shelton," he corrected. "Independently of the council. As the beasts weren't summoned by a Reaper and were taken care of, I see no reason for the council to get involved."

My mouth fell open. "Did you do that on purpose?"

"What do you think?" he said. "Do you really think I want the council sniffing around my house, forcing me to take on a new apprentice—or worse, bringing an outsider in?"

I stifled a laugh as he gave a theatrical shudder. He *had*

been looking out for me in a weird roundabout way. Okay, I could have done with a heads-up that there was a soul-eating monster in town, but as it was, we'd left no signs that might make it back to the other Reapers—if Shelton kept it quiet, that is, and it seemed Harold trusted him not to tell tales on me to the Reaper Council. In an indirect way, he'd actually done me a favour.

Wonders would never cease.

16

I wouldn't have minded celebrating upon my return to the inn, but instead, I went upstairs for a much-needed nap. I woke up when Drew texted me, letting me know that he'd dealt with Debora and the students and was on his way with an update. I barely had time to wake up properly before he knocked on the door to my room. I hastened to let him in, finding that unfortunately, he was wearing clothes by now. I guessed I couldn't have it all.

"I dropped Debora Lowe off in jail," he said. "The kids will probably be cautioned, too, and we've informed the parents."

"Is that it?" I asked. "The kids… I know they're only fifteen, but they could have got someone killed."

"I know," he said. "There's a limit to what we can do, and from what Shelton told me, the Reaper laws are much too harsh by our standards."

I grimaced. I almost felt sorry for those kids, for how they'd been manipulated and deceived. If not for the fact that their irrational hatred of Carey had led them into this to start off with, of course. If they hadn't been dead set on bringing down her ghost blog and humiliating her, they wouldn't have wound up falling for Debora's trickery. Then again, they were still kids, and the Reaper Council's punishments made a stint in jail look like a party.

"Did Debora Lowe offer an explanation for her hatred of the Reapers?" I sat back on the bed, fighting a new wave of exhaustion. Man, that fight had taken it out of me. "Except for her grudge against me for getting the former coven leader kicked out of town, I mean?"

"It sounds like she believed that your presence in town would cause all manner of buried crimes to rise to the surface," she said. "She's been watching you for a while."

"Wow," I said. "I'm flattered. Seems I make enemies without even trying. What kind of devious crimes was she trying to cover up, then?"

"Involvement with Mina Devlin, for one," he said. "When those kids went to her, looking for information on how to summon a ghost, she took the opportunity to deal with the issue herself by offering the suggestion of summoning up a hellbeast. I doubt she knew what she was dealing with. She said she got the spell from an old book."

"I should have known," I said. "Where is this book, anyway?"

"Shelton took it." An apologetic note entered his tone. "He said the Reaper Council would want it in their hands."

My mouth parted. "You know what? They can keep it. I'm better off without it in my life."

"I thought you'd say that," he said.

"What about Faith Murray?" I asked. "Did you let her out of jail?"

"I did, after a fashion," he said. "She's certainly got a temper, hasn't she? I think she and old Harold would get along well."

I grinned at that. "I have to speak to *him* again at some point, but I think I'll wait until tomorrow."

"Yes, you should sleep," he said in stern tones. "You've had quite enough excitement for one day."

"So bossy." I leaned back on the pillow to placate him and closed my eyes, unable to keep from grinning.

A moment later, something brushed my forehead. Had he just kissed me? I opened my eyes, only to see the door closing behind him.

That was something, though. It really was. I fell asleep with an even bigger grin on my lips.

———

The following morning, Carey was back at school, I was back at work, and Shelton the Reaper had vanished from town without so much as offering a goodbye. He stayed long enough to see justice served, and that was all. It'd have been nice if he'd thanked me for helping, but as long as he didn't say a word to the Reaper Council, he was welcome to do whatever he liked.

"I can't believe Harold called him here," I said to Mart as I worked my shift in the restaurant. "Without asking me first."

"In fairness, you couldn't have got rid of those monsters on your own," he said.

"Neither could he." Yes, I needed to get back into

practise with my Reaper skills, but without a scythe, that would prove tricky. Harold would not be thrilled at me if I asked to borrow his, but if something like this happened again, I'd need to be better prepared. Then again, I wasn't thrilled with old Harold either, and I fully intended to go to speak to him after my shift.

Carey came home from school that afternoon looking more upbeat than she had in a long time.

"How was it?" I asked.

"Good," she said. "Cris and the others are taking a few days off, but the rest of the class heard the whole story. They also heard about me swinging a scythe at the monster."

I grinned. "Which is true. They can't dispute the fact that you're way braver than they are."

With luck, Cris and her friends would have the sense to leave Carey alone from now on. She'd be able to do all the ghost hunting she liked without worrying about what they did.

Allie walked over to join us. "Everything okay?"

"Sure," said Carey. "The only problem is, a few more people at school have started reading my blog, and I need more content."

"Can't you have a week off ghost hunting?" said Allie. "I think you've already had enough excitement."

"Yes, but I'm not allowed to mention the hellbeasts, which means there's not much I can say publicly," she said with a glance at me.

"Yeah, we don't want the Reaper Council coming here after Shelton has already left," I said. "Pretty sure that isn't what old Harold wants either. But I'll come ghost hunting with you next weekend if you like. We'll pick somewhere relatively harmless."

Allie raised a brow at me. "Sure you aren't going out with the detective this weekend?"

"I don't know." I hadn't heard from him since he'd left my room yesterday. "I'll text him after my shift's over."

"Oh, never mind your shift," said Allie. "Leave early. Think of it as a reward for all you did for us. You can go and surprise the detective at work."

"Actually, I have somewhere else I need to go first," I said. "But thanks."

After leaving the inn, I made for the cemetery and Harold's cottage. When I knocked on the door, he yanked it open. "What?"

"I want to talk to you about Shelton."

"What about him?" he said.

"You called Shelton into town to get rid of those beasts," I said. "I understand why you didn't ask me to hunt the hellbeasts myself, but you might've *told* me they were lurking in the area. Then I wouldn't have been blindsided when they sneaked up on me."

"And you'd have left it alone, would you?" he said.

Well... no. Didn't mean I was happy about being left out of the loop when I'd been their intended target all along.

"No, she wouldn't," Mart supplied, appearing at my shoulder.

"Maybe not, but it would have been nice if I'd known what I was up against," I said. "Shelton couldn't handle three of them alone."

"I assumed it was only one," he said. "I didn't know the summoner would be foolish enough to summon three hellbeasts at once."

"Debora was fixated on hiding her secrets." I shook my head. "Pity it didn't work out for her in the end. How'd you find out the hellbeasts were here, anyway?"

"Faith Murray," he said. "She came to visit me when she found out what her co-worker was doing. She didn't have any proof, and she didn't want Mina Devlin's allies getting wind that she knew, so she came to me instead."

"Really?" I said. "That doesn't mean you couldn't have told me yourself. Why didn't *you* help Shelton?"

"I'm retired," he grunted. "Besides, someone has to make sure the spirits in this graveyard stay safe."

So he wanted to protect them. He really did care. He'd even gone as far as to protect my brother so there was no chance that he'd be devoured during my confrontation with the hellbeasts. I stifled a smile. "You know, there might be others in town who don't want a Reaper around. Debora wanted to cover up the coven's crimes, and to be honest, I'd like to know how many others were in on it."

His silence went on for a heartbeat too long.

"They did it, didn't they?" I said quietly. "The coven caused the floods."

The Reaper stepped back and slammed the door in my face. Then his raspy voice came from the crack in the door. "Don't you *ever* mention that to anyone aside from me. Not the witches nor even that detective friend of yours."

A chill raced down my back. "You *knew?* But—"

But the floods had killed his apprentice, along with a large number of the town's other inhabitants. How could he have let them get away with it?

"You overestimate my influence," he growled. "Especially over the witches. Driving the coven leader out of town won't be enough to put a stop to them."

"They even doctored the news reports from the time, didn't they?" I spoke more to myself than anything. Mina Devlin had written those reports. She'd tried to blame Ed James to divert attention from the real mystery… what had they been trying to do when the river had burst its banks? Was there a reason Eric hadn't been able to recall anything about his death?

"I'd advise you to forget all about it," old Harold answered. "And keep your mouth shut if you know what's good for you."

That was ominous. I suspected he wouldn't say more, so I turned away from the house. Then I jumped. Drew stood there, waiting for me, as though he'd known I'd be here.

I can't tell him. I couldn't risk him ending up being targeted, too. If Mina Devlin had doctored all the evidence from the time, would we ever find proof?

"Hey, Maura," he said. "I wondered if I'd find you here."

"We had unfinished business," I agreed. "I wanted to ask him what he was playing at when he called Shelton to town without telling anyone. I kind of understand why he did it, but he might've saved us a lot of trouble if he'd told me as well."

"You aren't wrong," he said. "Is there a chance the Reaper Council might show up in town?"

"You know, I'm not sure there is," I admitted. "Shelton isn't going to call them. That's why old Harold picked him to contact."

His brows shot up. "He did?"

"Looks like he wanted to make sure he wouldn't tell

tales on us," I said. "If he hadn't done that, I'd be a lot madder at him for hiding the truth from me."

"I understand that," he said. "Did Harold know anything more about the case? I think it's a shame that those two ghosts didn't get closure."

"They're together now, at least," I reminded him. "But now that you mention it, it's not a bad idea to go back to the news reports from the time and clarify that their deaths were caused by the floods and that Ed James was entirely innocent. I know most people don't know he was a suspect, but for his own peace of mind…"

"I'll see what I can do," he said. "I'd also be interested to see what comes out in Debora Lowe's hearing."

"Hmm." It caught my attention that Mart had vanished, leaving me alone with the detective. For now, I was all too happy to put all this behind us and move on. "Got any plans for tonight?"

Drew's brows rose. "I didn't, but if you're free…"

"I am." I slid my hand into his. "I can promise no Reapers will interrupt us this time."

We left the graveyard and walked away hand in hand. I couldn't say I'd entirely forgotten the threat of the absent coven leader hanging over our heads, but that didn't mean the old Reaper's pessimism would dictate my actions. I might not yet have a plan for how to deal with Mina Devlin if she returned, but that didn't mean I'd forget what she'd done.

If she came back to town, we'd be ready to meet her.

ABOUT THE AUTHOR

Elle Adams lives in the middle of England, where she spends most of her time reading an ever-growing mountain of books, planning her next adventure, or writing. Elle's books are humorous mysteries with a paranormal twist, packed with magical mayhem.

She also writes urban and contemporary fantasy novels as Emma L. Adams.

Find out more about Elle's books at: https://www.elleadamsauthor.com/

Find Elle on Facebook at https://www.facebook.com/pg/ElleAdamsAuthor/